"What d
Mr. Dumon⸻u
seem—
Irritation colored her face.

He appreciated her passion. With her face flushed and her eyes flashing midnight fire, he appreciated it a whole lot. But the subject was getting more serious than he cared for, reminding him he had a mission to accomplish. Beautiful *señorita* or not, he couldn't forget that.

"I resent being called a drifter on such short acquaintance," he said. "You know nothing about my plans."

"Plans?" She shrugged. "I, too, have those. But what is it you believe in?"

Jake stood and moved his gaze to Juan, Diego and then back to rest on hers. "*Señorita?* I believe in staying alive. Other than that? Not a damn thing."

She rose to her feet, her eyes shooting daggers. "Then you have no soul, Señor Dumont."

His brother had said as much the day he took off. Jake met her angry gaze with a sardonic smile. "I know."

* * *

The Rebel and the Lady
Harlequin® Historical #913—September 2008

Author Note

The history of the Alamo has always fascinated me, especially the stories of the Mexicans who fought beside the Anglo defenders against their own countrymen. Although my main characters are fictional, there are many real historical figures in this novel. Writing about the Alamo cannot be done without mentioning Travis, Bowie, Crockett, Seguín—or General Antonio López de Santa Anna. The part played by Francita Alavez, the young woman in Goliad, is also well documented. It is with utmost respect that I have included them in my story, keeping as historically accurate as my research allowed. Any errors are completely mine.

I love to hear from my readers. You can reach me at P.O. Box 606, Rockton IL 61072 or contact me through my Web site at www.kathrynalbright.com.

Happy reading!

Kathryn

THE *Rebel and the Lady*

KATHRYN ALBRIGHT

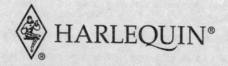

TORONTO • NEW YORK • LONDON
AMSTERDAM • PARIS • SYDNEY • HAMBURG
STOCKHOLM • ATHENS • TOKYO • MILAN • MADRID
PRAGUE • WARSAW • BUDAPEST • AUCKLAND

ISBN-13: 978-0-373-29513-5
ISBN-10:   0-373-29513-8

THE REBEL AND THE LADY

This edition published by arrangement with Harlequin Books S.A.

® and TM are trademarks of the publisher. Trademarks indicated with ® are registered in the United States Patent and Trademark Office, the Canadian Trade Marks Office and in other countries.

www.eHarlequin.com

Printed in U.S.A.

Available from Harlequin® Historical and
KATHRYN ALBRIGHT

The Angel and the Outlaw #876
The Rebel and the Lady #913

**DON'T MISS THESE OTHER
NOVELS AVAILABLE NOW:**

#911 THE SHOCKING LORD STANDON—Louise Allen

Encountering a respectable governess in scandalizing circumstances,
Gareth Morant, Earl of Standon, demands her help. He educates
the buttoned-up Miss Jessica Gifford in the courtesan's arts.
But he hasn't bargained on such an ardent, clever pupil—
or on his passionate response to her!
The next sensual installment of Louise Allen's
***Those Scandalous Ravenhursts** miniseries!*

#912 UNLACING LILLY—Gail Ranstrom

Abducting Lillian O'Rourke from the altar is part of his
plan of revenge. But Devlin Farrell has no idea that he will
fall for his innocent captive. Devlin may be baseborn,
but to Lilly he's the truest and bravest gentleman....
A dramatic tale of love, danger and sacrifice.

#914 TEMPLAR KNIGHT, FORBIDDEN BRIDE— Lynna Banning

Beautiful, talented Leonor de Balenguer y Hassam
is more interested in music than marriage, while
Templar Knight Reynaud is seeking his true identity.
As they travel together, both keeping secrets, attraction flares,
but Reynaud knows he can't offer Leonor what she deserves....
Travel on a thrilling journey through medieval France and Spain!

For my husband, Dean, who loves stories of the
West as much as I do.
Here's your Western, honey….

Chapter One

January, 1836—Southern Texas Territory

The ground shook.

Victoria Torrez jerked awake from a dreamless sleep and glanced about her room. Nothing was out of place. The full moon shining through her window cast shadows of bare branches on the plaster walls. What had woken her?

She swung her feet onto the tile floor and tiptoed to the window. Nothing moved in the blue moonlight. A heavy frost covered the ground near the hacienda, unusual for this time of year, but then it had been an unusually cold, dry winter. The bats that lived along the Rio Grande had long since flown south. Even the owl that hooted in the ancient oak tree was still.

Too quiet.

Her senses heightened, she moved to the opposite window to search the courtyard.

It came to her then—a steady, rhythmic trembling like thunder in the wake of an approaching storm. Her heart took up the cadence as she held her breath and listened, trying to understand what was happening.

The iron latch on her door jiggled. "Victoria? Wake up!" her mother urged with a frantic edge to her voice as she stepped into the room.

Grabbing her robe from the back of a chair and stuffing her arms into the sleeves, Victoria secured the tie around her waist. "I'm awake. What is it?"

"El Presidente has come."

Victoria's stomach lurched. "No! Santa Anna? It cannot be!" Then soldiers marched across their land! How many must there be to make the ground tremble?

Mama joined her and together they peered outside.

Victoria's father stood on the far side of the ornate iron gate that closed off the courtyard. His back was to them, and although he'd dressed hastily with his shirt hanging loose rather than tucked into his *pantalones,* his stance was wide and proud. His breath rose, a warm vapor in the cold air, as he spoke to another man who held himself tall, chin up, his feathered hat tucked in his arm. The stranger wore a dark uniform with brass buttons that gleamed in the moonlight and a sword at his side. Not Santa Anna. She had seen a painting of El Presidente once when she visited Monterrey. Perhaps this was an emissary.

Behind him, she could barely make out the gray

forms of more soldiers standing in rows. With the low mist creeping from the river, her eyes failed to see beyond the third line of men, but there must be more. From what she'd heard, the general's army was vast.

The two men spoke softly at first and Victoria could hear only the low tones, unable to differentiate the words. Then their voices rose to an angered pitch. Her heart thumped hard in her chest, worried that next they would come to blows or worse. A heavy silence hovered while each man weighed the other's intent. After a moment, the officer bowed stiffly and retreated. Her father turned away, an uncharacteristic slump to his shoulders.

This couldn't be happening! "Santa Anna was to come in the spring—and by boat," Victoria murmured, still unable to believe what was before her.

"We will not see Monterrey now," Mama said, her hands clasped and trembling around her beaded rosary.

Father had planned to take the family safely to his brother's house before the army came. Victoria had spoken against it. She did not want to leave the cattle and horses to be used by the Mexican army. She would not hand over anything to them so easily.

Heavy footsteps in the great hall startled them both. Mama stepped forward and wrapped the ends of her heavy shawl across her chest, a five-foot, one-inch formidable fortress. Searching for a quick weapon, Victoria grabbed the silver letter opener from her writing desk and hid it within the folds of her robe. She moved next to her mother. Steadying her breathing, she prayed fervently the intruder was simply their cook.

The door swung open.

"Esteban!" His name rushed from her lips as she recognized her childhood friend. His face was more angular now, more mature than when she'd last seen him in the summer. "What are you doing here?" The moment the words were uttered she realized he wore a soldier's uniform and carried a pistol in his hand. A sinking sensation settled in her chest. He'd joined the Mexican army.

Darting a quick look around the bedroom he strode toward them, the sharp planes of his face stern. "Señora Torrez, Victoria—you must get out of here."

"But this is my home," Victoria said, raising her chin. "I will fight for it."

His dark eyes flashed as he gripped her shoulders with his long fingers. "I have seen the army. There are too many coming."

"And you have made it one more." She shrugged out of his grasp, not caring that the anger in her voice was audible. How dare he do this! And now she realized the clothes he wore were not those of a common soldier. From the crown of the golden helmet protecting his head all the way to the bottom of his polished black leather boots, authority oozed from every inch of him. Gold epaulets padded both shoulders of his dark blue coat and a sword with a brass hilt hung from his belt. Of course that would be the way of it. He was not a common man, after all, but one of the aristocracy of Mexico.

"Why, Esteban? Why did you do such a thing? You come now to fight against my family and steal our land? Land that has been ours for generations."

His closed expression gave his answer before he spoke. "You had a chance to save this land, and gain more besides. But you refused me, remember? My offer of marriage did not agree with you."

Beneath his hard facade she could see the hurt her rejection had caused. In his eyes she caught a glimmer of what looked like…hope.

Even now.

"I explained my reason. I will not have my future arranged for me. I will choose my own husband."

"Your father has been too lenient with you."

"I am his only child. Can you blame him for doting? I know you, Esteban. You would do the same with your daughter." She'd hoped by being honest they could remain friends. She cared for him—but as a brother.

Moving to her bureau, she opened a small drawer and removed the engagement ring he had given her on her twenty-first birthday. She held it out until he reluctantly raised his hand for it. As she folded his fingers around the cold metal with her own she beseeched him. "You have always been a good friend. Do not ruin that now."

For a moment he struggled with her answer, but then with his hand resting on the brass hilt of his sword, he hardened his jaw. "Now I choose my own path. In honor of my gentleman status, El Presidente has given me a commission in his army. I command a contingent of dragoons."

"Then you had better get back to them," a deep voice said from behind him.

Esteban spun around, whipping up his pistol as he turned.

"No!" Victoria jumped forward, pushing the gun to the side. "What are you doing? You know my father! Often you have sat at our table."

Esteban pushed her aside, out of his way, but never lost sight of the man before him. "Stay back." He brought his gun back up and trained it on the man before him.

Her father spoke first, his voice calm but steely. "Do you come as a friend to this house, Esteban? Or as the enemy?"

The air charged with electricity as they faced each other—a Tejano believing Tejas deserved its freedom, and a Mexican patriot trying to quell a rebellious uprising, one that threatened to split the country in two. There would never be a middle ground. The time for that had passed long ago.

Slowly, cautiously, Esteban holstered his gun and removed his hat, tucking it under his arm. Then, in the way of the dons, gentleman to gentleman, he bowed to her father. "Señor Torrez. It is with relief that I find you well."

"And you, too, Esteban Castillo," Father said, making an equally cautious bow.

"Surely you understand the danger of the situation. You are no longer a young man and there are too many soldiers for you to fight."

"Your General Romero has asked politely enough

if his army can camp on my land, eat my grain and slaughter my livestock. He, of course, wants the hacienda for himself and his officers. I suppose that means you." Sarcasm thickened her father's voice.

"If you agree to this, he will count you as loyal to Santa Anna and leave you unharmed with only the loss of a few chickens. Refuse him, and you and your family are dead."

"I understand these things," Father growled. "I have considered long on what could happen should he come here, but I was not prepared to see him in winter. What general marches his soldiers at winter's end when there is little stored grain for food and little protection from the weather?"

"One who understands the use of surprise as a weapon."

Father's gaze was cold. "Or one who cares little for those he commands." He turned to contemplate Mama and then her, his face drawn. "I thought he would come by boat, not march so many across this harsh land."

She stepped forward, afraid for what she saw in his eyes—so close to despair. "Your way made more sense, Papa." She took his hand.

"I thought there was time to take my family to safety in the spring." He placed his free hand over hers and squeezed. Searching her face, his gaze lighted on her with love—and worry. "But now there is no time."

Esteban watched him dispassionately. "Then you know what you must do."

Father's jaw clenched. "I will do what I must to survive this. To keep my family safe."

"What are you saying?" Victoria asked. Father was a proud man. He believed in the cause—a free Texas. They had talked of it often in his study and when riding across the ranch together.

He released her hand. "We will submit."

"You would give up everything to protect us?"

She couldn't let that happen. His dream was her dream. She loved this land. She couldn't let him give up his beliefs because of worry for her. "No, Papa. Commancheros, droughts, fires—there have been many enemies over the years. Santa Anna is but one more."

"A most formidable one," Father said, his slight smile only for her. "Don't worry, *pequeñita.* I can fight another day."

At overhearing the words, Esteban's brow furrowed. "You must not say such things or when next we meet, one of us will have to kill the other. I do not want to be that man."

Father turned, shielding her with his body from Esteban. "We must all choose our side. You have not told me anything I did not already know. Which makes me wonder again—why are you here?"

Esteban smoothed the feathered plume on his helmet as he considered his reply. With a glance in Victoria's direction, he said, "Please, *señor,* I know your daughter will not have me as her husband." He swallowed hard. "I must respect her decision in this, but still I do not wish to see her hurt. You cannot protect her. Not against so many. And once the officers see her…" The words trailed off, and he struggled with finishing his thoughts. "She is a rare beauty, Señor Torrez. I…I am afraid for her."

The letter opener dropped from her hand unheeded and clattered to the floor as a new fear rose up inside her. The officers would not dare to touch her, would they? She was no camp follower. Her lineage could be traced back nine generations to the Acalde in Madrid, Spain.

"So your general makes war on women?" her father said.

"No. Of course not. But Victoria is beyond compare. And Santa Anna has…appetites. I…I am afraid for her," he repeated awkwardly. A slight flush came to his cheeks.

"Then what do you propose?"

"To take her far from here—as far away from the fighting as possible."

Victoria couldn't believe he would separate her from her family. She needed to stay here and help. "That is impossible, Esteban!"

Father turned to her and studied her face, lifting the point of her chin with his fingers.

Shocked that he would consider Esteban's words, she grasped his forearm. "No! I wish to stay with you. I am strong. I can fight."

His gaze hardened. "In this, Victoria, you will do as I say."

"Father," she said once more, "do not send me away."

Her father gave little indication that he heard her, instead he turned to Esteban. "Where would you go? Where does the army go next?"

Esteban looked affronted. "I cannot tell you that!"

"You're an officer," her father pressed. "Surely you know Santa Anna's plans."

"Even if I knew, I would not tell you. You would make a traitor of me when I am here to help you."

A slight nod was the only indication her father understood the truth of Esteban's words.

Esteban thought for a moment. "Where does she have family?"

"Monterrey."

"Too far. I cannot leave my men for that long. Is there no one closer?"

Father looked at Mama and silent communication seemed to flow between them. "Your cousin, Gertrudis? Juan and his family?"

Mama nodded, but there were tears in her eyes. "Bejar. The Texians have control of the city now. Perhaps she will be safe at their hacienda until we can bring her back."

It didn't make any sense to Victoria. She moved closer to whisper in her father's ear. "But, Papa. If the Texians are in control, surely that will be where Santa Anna goes next?"

Under the guise of a bracing hug, she felt his slight nod. "Go to Juan," he said softly, urgently. "His family is well thought of in Bejar. He will be able to protect you."

Papa let go and turned to Esteban. "You will

escort her there? I have your word as a gentleman that you would guard her honor?"

With a formal bow and a click together of his boot heels, Esteban answered solemnly. "With my life."

She barely heard his answer. The strange look between her parents, the things her mother said— what was it that they wanted of her? It dawned on her then. She must warn her cousin Juan that Santa Anna was near, so that the people of Bejar could prepare themselves. Excitement thrummed through her.

Didn't Esteban understand? She tried to keep the urgency from showing on her face. Was he so intent on getting her to safety that he hadn't evaluated the consequences? Or, more likely, did he suspect that she, being a woman, gave such things little thought?

"You must trust me, Victoria," Esteban said, mistaking her hesitation for fear. He started to leave, but at the door he stopped. "Wear dark clothes. Pack only what you can carry on your horse and meet me in the stable in fifteen minutes." He walked through the doorway.

She turned to her parents. "I will warn Juan. You can count on me, Papa."

"The journey will not be easy," he said, a worried look on his brow. He crossed to her writing desk and withdrew a sliver of paper, and then dashed off a quick note. Straightening, he blew on the indigo ink and then folded and handed it to Victoria. "This tells the approximate size of the army and the names of the generals here, but you must let Juan know there are two other armies to the south gaining ground. He must prepare immediately."

She tucked the paper in her fist and glanced between her mother and father. "What will become of you?"

Father shook his head. "For now I'll do as the soldiers ask. This General Romero appears to be a respectable man. I do not think we will come to harm."

He folded her into a hug, and she drew in the scent that was his alone, mixed with the tobacco of his favorite cigar. "Get dressed now. There is little time."

She turned to her mother. "Mama," she murmured, wrapping her arms around the woman's neck and shoulders.

"Vaya con Dios," her mother said, tears wetting her face. "Be strong." With an extra squeeze, she let go and stepped away.

A lump formed in Victoria's throat. Would she ever see her family again? She could not allow herself to believe otherwise. She clamped her teeth together, afraid her parents would see her trembling. She must be strong as her mother said—strong and resilient. Pulling herself up tall, her shoulders back, she memorized her parents' proud faces. "A Torrez has safeguarded this land for generations. Now it is my turn and I am ready. I will make you proud."

The first night of their journey north, when Victoria dismounted from her horse, her legs would not obey her. She crumpled to the ground, and only the mare's intelligence, or perhaps its weariness, kept the beast from trampling her. As conditioned to riding as Victoria had been all her life, she still ached in places she did not know could hurt—her thighs, her knees, her hips. Esteban treated her with courtesy and care but dared not slow his pace to accommodate her. She wouldn't have wanted it, anyway. She had to get to Juan to warn him. If only her body was as strong as her resolve.

Late into the night of the fifth day, they reached the town of San Antonio de Bejar. The moon cast the church tower and adobe houses in a pale-blue light, the sight surreal in her state of exhaustion. Her eyes kept drifting shut as she struggled to stay in her saddle. Sleeplessness and the aches and pains from the trail had taken their toll. She could barely keep Esteban in her vision. He sat taller in the saddle, alert for trouble as they entered the small town. He'd changed from his soldier uniform into a cotton shirt and canvas pants for the journey. The common peasant clothes along with a serape made it possible for him to ride all the way to her cousin's door without being challenged. She glanced around, aware for the first time that no one had stopped them, no one had questioned them.

Guards should be posted. The soldiers had no idea that Santa Anna was so close—right on her heels. Things would change once she spoke with Juan. She was sure of it.

Her horse stumbled. She grabbed a hank of mane

and adjusted herself in the saddle, as her eyes drifted closed again. The sound of subdued voices carried to her. Vaguely it registered that Esteban had dismounted and talked quietly to a couple in the doorway of an adobe house. They were dressed in their night clothes. She looked up at the starlit sky with the dipper constellation overhead so large and clear. How late was it? A chill went through her and she gathered her heavy cloak closer.

Esteban led her mare down the street and they stopped before another house. A man stepped through the large doorway—her cousin, Juan.

She hurried to dismount, feeling Juan's firm hands helping her at the last. She turned to face him. Drawn and worried, his face appeared older by more than the passage of two years since she'd last seen him. "The soldiers…you must warn them…" Her tongue, thick and dry, did not want to work.

"You are a long way from home, *prima*. Come inside and tell me what has happened."

"Esteban…" She remembered her manners.

Juan's lips pressed to together. "He is already getting some food from my cook and then will be on his way."

"You will let him go? He will not come to harm?"

Juan nodded. "Yes. Although I am afraid he has seen how unprepared we are here and will take that information with him for his own use and that of the Santanistas."

"We will prepare. We will tell the soldiers at the fort."

Her cousin opened his mouth to say more, but then clamped it shut, his jaw tightening.

"What is it?" she asked.

"You will learn soon enough. Come inside for now."

Chapter Two

Jake Dumont paced the length of the small room, trying to rein in his temper. Exhausted after traveling over half the country, he didn't need the setback Lieutenant Colonel Travis had just thrown in his path.

"What do you mean, he's gone?" Jake demanded. "Brandon came here to fight. He wouldn't turn tail."

"I'm not suggesting he has," the colonel said from his seat behind the small wooden desk. "Bowie sent him and another soldier to San Patricio five days ago."

"I was told you were in charge."

"I am—of the regular recruits. Jim Bowie heads the volunteers."

It was frustrating enough falling farther behind his brother due to the winter storm that blew through the Arkansas Territory with a vengeance, but then a day out of Béxar his horse had been startled by a cougar looking for an easy meal and had suffered an ugly clawing on his flank. To arrive and find he'd missed Brandon by less than a week had him ready to hit somebody.

He studied the map on Travis's desk, committing to memory the lay of the land and nearby towns. San Patricio was a far piece to the south.

"What is Brandon's assignment there?"

"To learn what he can of Santa Anna's whereabouts and gather more troops." Travis met his eyes over the hand-drawn map. "He failed to mention that he is a doctor. Didn't even ask about the hospital here."

"I don't think he has healing on his mind right now."

"No." Travis's stare was measuring. "I'd have to agree with you. Rather curious considering his chosen occupation. He was anxious to see some action. Perhaps I provided it for him."

Jake winced at the arrogant sound of that. Brandon didn't have any idea what he'd gotten himself into, but Jake did. And it wasn't all male camaraderie and whiskey. War changed a man, usually for the worse. Especially someone as idealistic as his brother. If Brandon couldn't see through the designs of one industrious female—the provocation for this foolhardy journey—he certainly wouldn't be able to comprehend the strategies of warfare and the manipulation of soldiers.

Noting Travis's perfectly fitted waistcoat and tailored white shirt, Jake wondered if someone so young and full of himself could actually hold the common soldier as important and necessary, or would he see him only as an expendable risk in one officer's rise up the ranks.

"What is the terrain like to San Patricio?" Jake asked, growing more concerned by the moment.

"Passable—if you follow the river rather than going straight overland. That will take extra time though. A good six days. And I don't have anyone extra to send with you."

Jake grunted. "Believe me, if I can find my way here from the Carolinas, I can get there without someone holding my hand." He rubbed the back of his neck as he considered his options. Fury needed to rest up if that gash was to heal. The horse would obey whatever Jake asked, but that didn't mean Jake would ride the beast into the ground. Maybe he could leave in a few days and still catch up to Brandon.

A knock at the door sounded and two Tejanos entered the room. One appeared close to Jake's age of twenty-eight and had the bearing of an officer, although he wore no uniform. Instead, with the split-legged trousers and striped poncho, Jake pegged him as a land owner of some merit. He removed his wide-brimmed hat and held it before him, waiting for permission to speak.

The other looked younger—not quite a man yet, but nearly there judging by the fuzz on his upper lip. His build was slender and bony at the hands and shoulders. He swiped off his hat, stained with grime and sweat, as he stepped up to the desk.

Travis rose from his seat. "Captain Seguín. Diego. Good. You're back." He turned to Jake, a new urgency in his voice. "Look—your brother will be back by the end of next week. Why don't you relax. Rest up a bit. We're having a party at the cantina tomorrow night celebrating Washington's birthday."

Jake raised his brows. "This isn't the United States."

"But there are plenty of men from the States here itching for something to combat the boredom. A party should do it. Come have a drink with us."

It was tempting, Jake thought as he rubbed his scruffy neck again. A shave. A bath. Besides, that mean-looking gash on Fury's flank had started to fester. He'd stitched it up as best he could, but it was oozing a nasty-smelling discharge. He needed to take care of it. "I might still be here. Where can I find the apothecary?"

"Hospital is up at the fort. Talk to Dr. Pollard. You'll find lodging there, too—for you and your horse."

Victoria walked down the street carrying a kettle of chicken soup and grumbling to herself. She had been to the edge of town that morning and still there were no soldiers posted as lookouts. Didn't the officers understand how close Santa Anna's army was? Why did they not prepare? It had been four days since she'd arrived in town. She'd expected to help Juan secure his house here and move into the fort—and perhaps prepare the women. No one took her warnings seriously except Juan.

She glanced down at the heavy iron pot she held. All she'd done so far was take food to the hospital in Maria's stead—not nearly the action she'd desired. Juan had dismissed his cook after hearing the news Victoria brought, and smartly the woman had packed her things and headed back to her home west of town to warn her husband. The soldiers might enjoy this soup after the rations of corn tortillas they'd endured, but what would happen to the injured and ailing men once Santa Anna invaded the streets?

Again she worried about the lack of readiness. Shouldn't people be doing something? Preparing? It seemed a few Tejanos were, but not the stubborn and blind Americanos.

She strode past the barracks, making a beeline for the stairs to the hospital floor. Just as she mounted the first step, a dark blur of motion dashed out from under the stairway. The large mud-colored mongrel bounded toward her with its teeth bared, a rumbling growl in its throat.

"No!" she cried out, teetering on the brink of losing her balance as the dog dove into her skirt and between her legs. "No! Eyiee!" Hot soup sloshed out from under the kettle's lid and over the edge to burn her fingers. She would lose it all if she dropped it!

Suddenly a strong hand gripped the kettle and then grasped her elbow, steadying her. She looked up into a face that hadn't seen the sharp edge of a razor in weeks. His beard was the color of rich coffee but it couldn't hide the handsome contours beneath. Anglo, she reasoned. Easy to spot with the dark hair, streaked blond by the sun, and cobalt-blue eyes. His body tensed as he held tight to a ruff of fur at the dog's neck and pulled it away from her skirt. "Guess the smell of that soup was more than the poor mutt could take. You got that now?"

"Gracias," she said, gripping the kettle to her like a shield. Juan had warned her against being too familiar with the soldiers, saying they saw few women and were as uncouth a lot as he'd ever known. She sniffed. This man reeked of horse and sweat and days on the trail—not exactly a heady combination.

He tipped his hat. "Name's Jake. Jake Dumont."

"Gracias," she said again.

He was blocking her path. She started to sidestep to go around him but then he sidestepped and was in front of her again.

His eyes narrowed under his dark brows. "You don't speak English? A shame." His gaze slid over her, moving from the heavy blue cloak that covered her head all the way down to the base of her gray skirt where the tips of her boots peeked out. Angry heat flushed through her. He had nerve, this Anglo!

She raised her chin and gave him the haughtiest look she could muster under the circumstances. Repositioning her grip on the kettle, she started up the stairs, surprised when the man shoved the dog purposely to the side and followed her. She stopped and turned, putting the hot soup between them. If he thought to annoy her, she had plenty of protection.

He glanced at the soup and then back up at her. A

devilish look came into his eyes. "You think that would stop me?"

She tipped the kettle in warning. A drop of hot liquid splashed onto his pants.

Faster than lightning, he grasped her wrist. "Careful woman. There may come a day you won't want that part of me scalded."

Oh! He was a wicked man!

"Look. Let's not start a battle where there doesn't need to be one. I'm just going in the same direction as you—to see the doctor."

"You are sick?" He seemed like the last man on earth who'd be ill. His firm grip revealed only quick reflexes and crushing strength. Too late she realized her ruse was up. She'd spoken her thoughts out loud—in English.

He smiled slowly, his gaze knowing. "No. But my horse is."

Captured momentarily by the deep blue of his eyes, her heart thudded in her chest. He was different from anyone she'd known before and so sure of himself. Was this an American trait? She wasn't sure she liked it. It bordered on rudeness. They had not been properly introduced and here he was still touching her wrist.

As if he read her thoughts, he released her arm and took the kettle from her hands. "Relax, miss. Although you are the prettiest *señorita* I've ever had the pleasure of meeting, I've got other things on my mind at the moment." Then he passed by and continued up the stairs giving her a disconcerting view of his worn buckskin backside.

She frowned. She hadn't expected him to suddenly turn charming. Drawing up the hem of her skirt, she followed.

He crossed the room in half the number of strides it took her and set the kettle on a nearby table. Sick and injured men on pallets lined the interior walls. As she approached, the doctor looked up from his desk.

"Señorita Torrez. Thank you for thinking of my men again."

"They may all eat?" she asked. At his nod, she added, "There is plenty for you, too." By her count, the two open rooms that served as the hospital held nineteen patients. The aroma of onions and chicken filled the room as she ladled the soup into small bowls on the counter.

She felt the bearded man watching her. All these Anglos had such scruffy beards. They reminded her more of beasts or bears than men. The ones who were sick, she could understand, but the Mexicans she knew in Laredo kept theirs neatly trimmed or did not wear facial hair at all.

She sat down near the soldier on the end pallet and started spooning the food into his mouth, relieved to note the blue-eyed man turned away and started up a conversation with the doctor.

She didn't mean to listen, but couldn't help noticing the rich timbre of his voice. So pleasant and soothing. It called to her—resonating deep inside her. He had a slow and easy accent unfamiliar to her, and different from the other Anglos who lived here.

But he was too cocky for his own good. He wasn't to be trusted. A man like that usually took what he wanted and didn't worry about anyone else's feelings.

Still, she caught bits and pieces of their talk. He needed something for his horse. Something was infected. Well, at least he'd been telling her the truth about that.

She moved to the next patient, a man with his hands bandaged.

"Pssst!"

Startled, Victoria dribbled hot soup over the man's chest. "Oh! Pardon me!" She dabbed at the liquid with her apron before looking up from her work to find a woman motioning to her from the doorway of the room. *"Sí?"*

The woman glanced at the line of bedridden soldiers and at the doctor. She shook her head and made the sign of the cross over her breast.

"Excuse me," Victoria said to the man she'd been helping, and walked over to the door.

"Señorita," the woman said in Spanish. "Capitán Seguín is asking for you at the house."

"Did Diego return?"

"Sí."

Victoria's stomach clenched. This couldn't be good. She nodded to the woman. *"Gracias.* I will come immediately."

The woman left quickly, and Victoria turned back to the soldier on the pallet. She would not be able to finish helping him. The large Anglo had stopped talking to the doctor and watched her. Suspicion clouded his eyes. Just how much Spanish did he know? Had he understood the woman's words?

"Doctor Pollard? I am sorry to have to excuse myself. I have been called back to the house. I will come for the kettle later."

The doctor nodded to her and she turned and headed down the stairs, all the while feeling the other man's gaze on her. He filled the room with his rough presence and made her feel as though jumping beans were bouncing in her stomach. Not at all a pleasant sensation.

She crossed the small footbridge over the San Antonio River on her way back into town, drawing her cloak close about her shoulders. Loud voices came from inside the small general store as the door opened and a man stumbled out, his arms around a full sack of flour. He dropped it into a wagon loaded high with bedding and pans and tools. A woman held the bridle of the burro hitched to the cart and frequently scanned the street urging her husband to hurry.

Entering Juan's house, Victoria heard voices in the study. She stopped at the open door.

"Come. Victoria. You should hear this." Juan motioned for her to enter. He removed his hat and poncho and tossed them on a nearby chair. Apparently he had just arrived at the house himself.

She turned to Diego. He'd grown since she'd seen him last. Now, at eighteen, he stood taller than she and had become wiry. He wore an old leather hunting shirt, most likely from his father. "Welcome, Diego. I'm glad to see you here. What news do you bring?"

He nodded, his face serious. "Santa Anna's army is halfway between the Rio Grande and here. They're moving this way."

"How can that be when I left them at my father's hacienda just nine days ago? The soldiers are on foot, not riding as I did. They could not travel so fast."

"It is another section of the army, just as your father warned in his letter," Juan said. "I've told Travis."

"What is he going to do?" she asked.

"I don't know. He questions whether to believe me—a Tejano. I can see it in his eyes. He has not been in command long enough to understand how things are here. And he and Bowie don't agree on much." Juan pressed his lips together as he took Victoria's hands in his. "You came here for safety. I'm sorry."

"No, Juan. I came to warn you. To give you time to protect Gertrudis and your children. To help you prepare." Frustrated tears came to her eyes and she clenched her fist. "And now the soldiers linger and talk of parties instead of readying themselves."

Juan would not meet her eyes. "Perhaps I should help you leave town. I can't take you to my family as I wish to. They are already safely away. Perhaps the town of Mina…"

Trembling took hold of Victoria. She would not keep running. She had as much right to stay as they did. "I do not think there is a safe place left in Tejas. I will not go."

Juan's brow wrinkled in surprise. "No?"

"No. If you make me leave, I will slip away at the first chance and come back here. This is my fight, too."

"Victoria." He was frowning now. "I want to see you safe. Just as your father wanted. He gave you into my care. I do not take his wishes lightly."

She pulled herself to her full height. "I understand that, but this is my land, too—as much as it is my father's and mother's and yours. It is mine. Our people have given their blood and sweat to this land. Can I do less? My family is here. My place is here."

His gaze, although still worried for her, also held a measure of pride. He released her hands and nodded his agreement to let her stay. "So be it."

Turning to Diego, he continued. "I will talk to Travis. Perhaps he will grant leave to the men who have families and farms in Santa Anna's path."

"But, Juan," Diego said. "Your land is there, too. Will you go also?"

"No. I agree with our cousin. My place is here. I am captain. I must set an example."

Impulsively Victoria threw her arms around his neck and hugged him tight. Then she drew in Diego, too. "This will be where we stand."

Chapter Three

Jake heard the music coming from inside the cantina fifty paces from its doors. Someone played a violin and another a bass fiddle. Light from the candelabras inside spilled out in rectangular slashes onto the dirt street. When he opened the doors, the strong odors of smoke and beer assailed him. He glanced about the room, half hoping that he'd see the woman from the hospital. A pipe dream. Why would a beautiful *señorita* come to an American holiday celebration like Washington's Birthday?

He was no stranger to women from Mexico with their thick dark hair and their chocolate eyes, but he'd been flummoxed with her. When he had glanced from the dog up into her face, he'd actually been tongue-tied like a dull-witted greenhorn. She was that entrancing, with her dark eyes widened in surprise and that slightly shocked look on her face because he had dared to touch her, even though it was obvious he was trying to help. He'd thought at first her hair was black, slicked back as it was into a fancy coil at her neck. Then as the dog had her moving this way and that he saw that no, it was the darkest, richest shade of brown he'd ever seen.

And then he'd gone and goaded her. Unfortunately, he understood why. Guess he was just foolish enough to want to make an impression on her—even a poor one, if that's what it would take to get noticed. But damned if she hadn't come right back tilting that soup on him. He grinned just thinking about it—had caught himself stifling that grin half the day whenever the memory popped into his head. As proper as she appeared on the surface, underneath she was a handful—a challenge he couldn't ignore in spite of the fact he was only here one more day. She was an enticing splash of color in an otherwise drab and dusty town, and he wanted to see her again. He'd dressed as though she might show up, which meant he'd taken a bath, cut his hair and shaved. If she did appear, she probably wouldn't recognize him anyway.

Jake walked to the bar and watched a group of volunteers raise their mugs as one, guzzle down their beer and then slam their mugs on the table.

"Have fun tonight because we'll be out there again at daybreak if Bowie orders it," one man said.

"I'm too tired to heft my fork," complained another.

"That's not because you're tired, Ward. You're jest drunk."

"Maybe we should have thrown in with Travis instead." Ward continued to complain. "Digging a well isn't my idea of soldiering. Besides, there's no way we can defend this place."

Suddenly, a tall commanding figure in buckskin loomed over them. He slammed his fist on the table making the mugs jump an inch high off the table. "Hasn't anyone ever told you that the cockroaches in Mexico have ears?"

"This is Texas, Davey, uh, I mean Mr. Crockett." A young soldier reddened instantly.

"Not yet it ain't, but it will be." Crockett grinned at him, and then spoke in a quieter voice. "North side first. The rest of the walls will hold. And," he continued, his eyes narrowing on Ward, "Bowie might be ailing, but he ain't stupid. He's got his reasons for his orders." He straightened and headed for a table closer to the music—a table where Travis now sat.

Travis caught Jake's gaze and motioned for him to join them also.

Jake bought a shot of whiskey and then sat down with the lieutenant colonel.

"Glad you made it, Dumont. May I introduce David Crockett?"

Jake nodded to the man. He'd heard of him. "Enjoy your stint in congress?"

"Not enough to go back." Crockett took a swig from his mug of beer. "Lot of talk that didn't amount to anything."

"What are you doing here?"

"Same as everyone else. Looking for a piece of

heaven to stake a claim. Somewhere with good hunting and with bluebonnets that have an ear for good fiddlin'," he added with a wide grin. "And you?"

"Just passing through," Jake said noncommittally, glad when Crockett let the subject drop. He leaned back in his chair and relaxed. He was among his own element here and appreciated it. His recent visit home, if he had such a place anymore, had opened his eyes. Ten years was a long time to be gone from Charleston. He no longer fit in there—but then he never really had.

A boy stood on a nearby table and finished lighting the last of the candelabras overhead when a gust of cold air had the newly lit candles flickering wildly. Jake looked up to see what had caused the breeze. The view was like a gut punch. His *señorita*.

He couldn't take his eyes off her as she slipped the heavy blue cloak off her head and let it settle on her shoulders. A high silver comb held in place a black lace scarf over her hair knot, and small silver earrings shimmered daintily from each lobe. She wore a maroon silk dress trimmed with black bows that offered enough of a view of creamy skin at her throat to be enticing but not risqué. The material rustled in a very feminine way as she followed the man she came with, maneuvering gracefully between the tables and chairs. Another Tejano protected her from the back. Jake recognized the two as those he'd seen in Travis's office yesterday.

"Well, would you feast on that," Crockett said, letting a low whistle slip through his teeth.

"I am." Amusement laced Travis' voice. "And it

looks like every other young buck in this cantina is, too. Even Dumont here."

Crockett met Jake's gaze. "I didn't think Seguín would bring that cousin of his in here."

Jake's ears caught on the word *cousin* with a mixture of relief. Not her husband, then, or fiancé. "Why not?" he asked.

"You might use your eyes, Mr. Dumont," Travis said. "Look at her. Fine bones. She's not a mixture at all, she's a lady. Spanish aristocrat. Seguín's lineage goes way back. Someone like that usually is kept away from the commoners." He leaned forward as if to tell a great secret. "That would be us. This old cantina could get a bit rowdy for her."

"I get the feeling she can take care of herself," Jake said, thinking of his earlier encounter with her. At least she didn't have hot soup with her now.

Spying them, Juan made his way first to Travis's table and removed his hat. He was dressed well for such a dusty spot on the map, Jake thought as he glanced over the silver buttons on his shirt collar and the wide satin sash around his waist that matched the *señorita*'s dress.

"Any more news?" Juan asked in a low voice.

Travis shook his head.

Jake kept his gaze trained on the woman, wondering if she recognized him. If she did, she didn't acknowledge it.

Juan murmured something in Spanish to the young man with him and they headed to a table across the room.

As the others talked, Jake settled back in his chair and watched the woman. She radiated confidence and something else that tugged at him. The two men who sat with her laughed at something she said and he felt a stab of envy that they enjoyed her wit when he couldn't. She had charmed them to the point of being lapdogs—something he'd never let a woman do to him. He'd learned his lesson well. He raised his glass to an unseen past and caught the flash of her eyes as they met his. Quickly she looked away, raising her fan to her cover her face.

Crockett let out a laugh and slammed down his beer mug, spraying the table. "Dumont, you've got more guts than I took you for. She's way out of your league. She'll cut you down to size with that sharp hair comb of hers."

Jake motioned to a woman serving drinks at the next table.

"You're out of your mind, Dumont," Travis said. "Juan will never let you near her."

"All the better," he mumbled, wondering what the hell he was doing. "I'm up for a dare. Besides, I don't know that he'll have the final say."

"You're a cocky son of a gun," Crockett said. "It'll be entertaining to watch you get your balls mashed."

"Thanks for your overwhelming support."

The serving woman placed a glass of red wine in front of Señorita Torrez. She raised it to Juan, ready to thank him, only to see him scowl and shake his head. Searching the candlelit room, her gaze finally collided with Jake's and held. She recognized him all right. Awareness pulsed between them. He gave her his best lady-killer smile and rose from his seat, ready to join her. "Gentlemen?" he said by way of goodbye to his table partners. "It's been an education…"

She frowned and put the glass down. Then she pushed it to the farthest corner of the table.

Jake sat back down with a thump.

"You gonna let that stop you?" Crockett said, barely keeping the smirk from his face.

"Just a setback. She's playing hard to get."

Travis leaned forward. "What you don't seem to *get,* is that she's way out of your class."

"Nothing with skirts is out of my class. But I am choosy." He'd give her a few minutes, lull her back into thinking she'd get her way and that he'd given up.

"Thought you were heading out in the morning. Why are you interested in dallying with that filly when you're leaving for San Patricio?" Crockett asked.

Damned if he knew. Just something about her he couldn't let go. She lowered her fan slightly and he noticed a flush to her cheeks as another glance darted in his direction. Maybe she wasn't as immune to him as he'd thought. "My horse could use one more day to rest."

"You try the turpentine like Doc Pollard said?"

He nodded, turning his attention back to Travis. "Too early to tell if it's helping. Well, gentlemen, I'd like to stay and discuss things, but a challenge waits."

He raised his glass of whiskey. "To Washington— his great deeds, those remembered and those that aren't." He tossed the drink to the back of his throat, his courage bolstered by the liquid fire.

Half the room must have heard him. They all joined in with a hail of some kind. Then another man called out, "To freedom for Texas!" Tejanos and Texians alike raised their mugs. The band began a lively tune in the middle of the ruckus.

"Now you've started it," Crockett said with a grin.

The sound was deafening. Jake rose, dropped a couple coins on the table to pay for his drinks and headed over to the *señorita's* table.

As he approached, annoyance flitted across her face, quickly covered by a polite facade. Most women welcomed his interruption. This was a new experience—a diverting one, if nothing should come of it. When he stopped in front of her, she seemed reluctant to make the introductions to her cousin and the other man, Diego. However, they both stood and shook hands with him, remembering him from Travis's office.

"You know my cousin, Señor Dumont?" Juan asked.

"We met yesterday. I spoke with her outside the hospital."

Juan turned to the woman for an explanation. "You did not mention this."

"There was no need. It was nothing."

Jake raised his brows. "Nothing isn't exactly how I'd put it, Señorita Torrez. You nearly scalded me!" He caught Juan's eye. "And I won't be explaining where!"

Juan frowned and turned to her. "Victoria? Explain yourself."

Jake hid a quick smile. At least he'd learned her first name now, even though it had earned him a killer glare.

"Señor Dumont was kind enough to help shoo away a mongrel intent on the soup I carried to the hospital. I thanked him at the time. I did not expect to see him again."

"Soup?"

"For the injured men. Your cook asked me to take it. She could then get an earlier start to her home."

"It seems I owe you thanks," Juan said with all the finesse of a gentleman.

He did not invite Jake sit down with them. That being the situation, Jake charged ahead. "Instead of your gratitude, I'd rather have your permission to dance with the lady."

Juan raised his brows, and Jake could see him preparing a refusal.

"You don't need to worry about my intentions, Captain Seguín. I have none. I'm leaving the day after tomorrow as soon as my horse heals up. Just one dance—in honor of the occasion."

Her lips twitched at his last comment.

Encouraged by the reaction, he said again, "One dance. After all, it is a party."

"I am not swayed by this Washington celebration," she said. "I think you Anglos use it as an excuse to drink. However, if my cousin will allow it, I will consent to one dance."

More surprised by her acquiescence than he'd admit, Jake waited for Seguín's response. Finally the man nodded.

Diego frowned, rising to his feet. "You do not need to do this, Victoria."

"It is only one dance," she said as she stood. "And he was kind to help me yesterday. I probably would have dropped the soup and burnt myself if not for his quick action."

Jake shot a triumphant smile at her two body-guards and then followed her to the small open area used for dancing, his gaze on the seductive swaying of her gown. When she turned to face him, he looked into eyes the color of dark mahogany, fringed with long coal-black lashes and wondered at his good fortune—or perhaps her lack thereof. He raised his hand for her to take. "Bad pennies or *pezos* in this case."

With an elegant movement, she drew up the side of her skirt and then slowly placed her other hand in his. "*No entiendo.* I do not understand."

Despite her cool, smooth touch, he felt warmth rush up his arm. "They do turn up."

At his words, Victoria pressed her lips together. No matter her grimace, Jake found her tantalizing. At her best, she must be about five foot two, he figured. The top of her head reached his shoulder. She held herself in rigid control as she followed his lead, and still she was the most graceful thing on the dance floor.

"Relax, Victoria. Unlike the dog earlier today, I won't bite."

She scowled. "You use my given name freely."

"It's a beautiful name—like you."

That earned him another frown. Was she really so used to men who took a year to say hello? Well, he wouldn't change to suit her. He didn't have the inclination or the time. "I take it the dog hasn't bothered you again?"

"No, *señor.* After you handled the situation, it gave up completely."

He smiled. "I have that influence at times."

She caught the innuendo and gave him a slow, assessing look. "You are a very confident man."

"Persistent, too. I don't take no for an answer, but a challenge." He swirled her around the small floor, enjoying the feel of her in his arms. She followed his lead effortlessly, her eyes taking on a shine. She *was* enjoying this, even if she wouldn't admit it.

"An answer to what question?"

He stared at her full lips. "Why, what every man here is wondering as they watch us dance."

She raised a dainty, perfectly arched brow.

"Will the lady allow him a kiss?"

Her lips pressed together again, this time stifling a smile that threatened.

He knew he was being forward—cavalier by any woman's definition, but his mood had lifted considerably when she'd consented to the waltz. After all, it was all about the chase, and she seemed to be enjoying it. With effort he dragged his gaze away from her lips and focused on her eyes.

"With you, I think the answer I seek—" he leaned

close, close enough to be tickled by a few wisps of her hair, and whispered into her ear "—is a yes."

She stiffened slightly within his arms.

"I'll take care of that later, darlin'."

"You are too bold, *señor.* Perhaps I would consider a kiss if you could ask for it in my language. Until then, my answer is no."

He grunted.

A smug smile lifted her lips.

Oh, she was tempting, definitely tempting enough to learn a few phrases. "How many kisses? Surely a phrase is worth more than one kiss?"

"For now, let's just enjoy the dance."

Her breath came in shorter gasps as he twirled her around, making sure to keep her just this side of dizzy. She relaxed the rigid hold she had on her body, her cheeks flushing with color, as she let herself enjoy the music.

"That's better," he said, drawing her close again and breathing in the perfumed soap she'd used earlier in the day. "Now, tell me what brings you here to this cow town in the middle of winter."

She gave him a sweet, evasive smile. "A visit with my cousin, of course."

"You expect me to believe that?" He paused, studying her face—the straight classic nose, the large smoky eyes. That she couldn't meet his gaze gave him his answer, but she sure was striking when she was telling a tale.

"Of course I do."

"What if I said I thought you were lying?"

She faltered in her steps. "You do not know me well enough to say whether I am or not."

"True—and I'd never argue with such a beautiful *señorita,* but still you haven't given me the entire truth."

The mysterious half smile she bestowed upon him made him catch his breath. "And why should I pour out my heart to you when you will be gone once your horse has healed?"

The candlelight reflected on the soft contours of her face as he drew her closer. "I can only think of one reason."

Her gaze dropped to his mouth.

Damned if she wasn't curious! Tempted even. Anticipation had him pulling her nearer. Maybe she'd consider dropping the Spanish lesson after all.

"The music has stopped, Señor Dumont."

Her words were like the shake of a rattler's tail—stopping him cold. He looked up to find the men in the band heatedly discussing their next song. He swallowed hard. "So it has," he said, surprised at what he'd been about to do. It wasn't like him to lose track of his surroundings. He'd been ready to kiss her right there on the dance floor in front of everyone. A foolhardy thing to do considering her status. The men with her would probably demand a duel or, God forbid, marriage at such an overture.

"If I had let you kiss me, I would have had to slap you, to keep my honor."

"It would have been worth it."

Her dark eyes sparkled.

Confidence surged through him. He was enjoying this. For the first time in a long while he was with a woman he could respect and appreciate. Better to keep her off balance with a little cockiness than to let her think he was serious. He was the last person she should get serious about. "One more turn about the floor?"

"Victoria?" Juan said from behind him, his voice stern. "Come back to the table now."

She looked at her cousin, then back to him, and stepped from his arms. "*Sí*. Thank you for the dance, Señor Dumont." Her head high, she placed her hand on Juan's arm. "Would you care to join us?"

Surprised, his gaze shifted to Juan. The man was not pleased with her request but was too polite to argue.

"You may tell us about your poor horse," she continued, and with a beguiling smile in his direction, she headed back to the table where Diego waited.

His horse was the last thing on Jake's mind at the moment. He watched as Victoria disappeared in the midst of the other dancers on her way across the room. Here was a challenge he couldn't refuse even though it led nowhere. She fascinated him, and apparently she wasn't completely immune to him, either. He followed her back to the table and settled into the chair across from her.

Captain Seguín motioned for a round of drinks. He waited until the waitress had deposited the mugs of ale and for Victoria, wine. "What is this about your horse?"

The man was just being polite, feigning interest, but Jake appreciated that it was for Victoria's sake. "I was a day out of town when a cougar startled me and attacked my horse. It clawed his flank. I fired a shot to scare it off."

"You are lucky it did not hurt you, as well."

Jake agreed, nodding. "I stitched up the gash as best I could, but it looks to be infected now."

"What have you used on it?" Victoria asked.

"The doc said to try turpentine."

She wrinkled her nose and he heard the word *barbaric* from Diego.

Juan watched him, his gaze steady.

"Doc Pollard said there's no more medicine for the men, let alone animals. And turpentine was the only thing he could think of that might work, other than warm compresses and prayer."

"He ran out of any strong medicine over two months ago," Diego said, leaning his chair back on two legs. "We're going to need it, too." The party-like atmosphere evaporated around the table.

"Why are we even here, Juan?" Victoria asked, setting down her glass. "With Santa Anna so close, why are we sitting in a cantina with all these Anglos and celebrating an American named Washington? It makes no sense to me. Why aren't the soldiers preparing for battle?"

With a glance at Jake, her cousin shook his head at Victoria.

He's afraid to say anything with me at the table, Jake realized. "I'd be interested in the answer to that, too," he said. "My brother came here to join the rebels."

Seguín studied him a moment, then leaned forward and lowered his voice. "When Diego returned from scouting south of here, he told Travis how close the Mexican army was but the man has turned a deaf ear. I think he is unable to take the word of a Tejano, even one who will fight at his side."

The news worried Jake. Wasn't San Patricio to the south? He tried to remember the map in Travis's office. "Why are you staying, then? Half the town looks deserted. What makes you stay?"

"My home is here," Juan said. "It has belonged to my family for generations. The Mexican government does nothing to protect it from the Commancheros. Santa Anna takes our money in taxes but he does not care for the land or its people. I stay because I will fight for an independent Tejas."

A proud light stole into Victoria's eyes. "Juan has raised his own force and has his commission from Commander in Chief Austin. He and Diego will not back away from this and neither will I."

Jake fingered the handle on his mug and tried to imagine caring about his home the way these two seemed to. "And this land of Juan's…is it yours, too?"

"No." She hesitated, but then continued. "My family's land lies farther south, near the Rio Grande."

She is beautiful, Jake realized, even more so with the zeal of misguided loyalty shining in her eyes. This cause would only bring her despair. He wanted to shake some sense into her. Land wasn't worth dying for. He'd said as much to his brother when Brandon had brought up the subject.

Diego tipped his beer toward Jake. "Yesterday, in his office, Travis said you were good with a gun. What do you carry?"

"A .40 caliber flintlock—a Dickert."

Diego gaze shifted to Juan, apparently impressed with the rifle.

"It's a good shot… 270-300-yard accuracy."

Diego snorted. "A rifle is only as true as the man who aims it. Where did you learn to shoot?"

"I've done a bit of hunting in my time, and scouting. My accuracy is what kept me alive." He looked from Juan to Victoria, not liking the speculation in their eyes. He didn't like to let loose about himself. "This some kind of test?"

"Of course not," Juan said smoothly.

Diego's innocent enthusiasm belied Juan's words. "Are you joining with us also?"

Jake wondered who that "us" was. Did Diego include Anglos and Mexicans together? He hadn't gotten that impression when talking to Travis. It seemed that the American immigrants wouldn't turn away help, but they were in it for themselves either to protect the land they'd homesteaded over the years or to section off a parcel for themselves. He couldn't blame them for that but it didn't matter to him. He wasn't fighting anyone. "I'll shoot if I have to, to stay alive, but I'm not joining up."

"Then why have you come here?" Victoria asked.

"To get my brother."

"And he is here?" Victoria asked, looking around the room.

"He was. Bowie sent him to San Patricio a week ago. He's supposed to be back soon but I think I'll head that way and catch up to him. He's just young enough and green enough to want to talk with this Santa Anna and strike a bargain."

Juan raised a brow. "Negotiate? It has been tried before. Santa Anna will throw him in jail before he finishes his first sentence in Spanish. He does not negotiate with Anglos. Look what happened to Austin."

"Exactly," Jake said. "Brandon doesn't stand a chance against such a man."

"What will you do when you find him?" Victoria asked.

"Drag his bony butt back home to South Carolina. He has a fiancée waiting there for him. I promised her I'd bring him home." In his opinion she wasn't worth the paper Brandon had written his goodbye note on, but that was another matter he'd have to discuss with his brother. He looked up to find Victoria studying him.

"Why don't you both stay? Stay and help us," she urged.

"Victoria," Juan said, a note of warning creeping into his voice. "Señor Dumont must do what he thinks right."

Her eyes sparked. "But if he's good with a rifle we could use him!"

"This is our fight, not his," Juan said. "We need people who believe in what they're fighting for."

Irritation colored her face. "What do you believe

in, then, Mr. Dumont? Or are you just as you seem—
a shiftless drifter?"

He didn't care for her appraisal of him but he did
appreciate her passion. With her face flushed and her
eyes flashing midnight fire, he appreciated it a whole
lot. But the subject was getting more serious than he
cared for, reminding him he had a mission to accomplish. Beautiful *señorita* or not, he couldn't forget
that.

"I resent being called a drifter on such short acquaintance," he said. "You know nothing about my
plans."

"Plans?" She shrugged. "I too have those. But
what is it you believe in?"

Jake stood, and moved his gaze to Juan, Diego
and then back to rest on hers. "*Señorita?* I believe in
staying alive. Other than that? Not a damn thing."

She rose to her feet, her eyes shooting daggers.
"Then you have no soul, Señor Dumont."

His brother had said as much the day he took off.
Jake met her angry gaze with a sardonic smile. "I
know."

Chapter Four

The next morning Victoria headed to the hospital, determined to put Jake Dumont out of her mind—not an easy task. Whenever she thought of him, she remembered the way her heart had raced while dancing and how safe she had felt in his strong arms. Never had she met a man so sure of himself, so sure of his ability to get what he wanted. And for a moment last night, it seemed he wanted her.

With a quick sign of the cross over her breast she thanked God she had found out his true character—selfish and arrogant. That she had even contemplated what his kiss would be like upset her now. She'd looked at his lips and heat raced up her cheeks. And he had known what she was thinking. That irked her all the more.

Today it was good there were more important needs to occupy her thoughts.

When she entered the hospital, Dr. Pollard was

engrossed in a conversation with another man. He noticed her entrance and introduced her.

"This is Doctor Southerland, Miss Torrez. John, Miss Torrez is new in town. Her cousin, Juan, is in charge of the Tejano regiment."

She murmured a greeting. "I am here to collect the soup kettle."

"Of course. It's there on the table. Thank you." He turned back to his conversation as she walked across the room. "I'd like you to look at Bowie, John. I'm not sure if it's pneumonia or maybe something else."

"Be happy to. Where is he?"

"He has moved into the fort. I'll take you to him."

Victoria picked up the empty kettle and followed them down the stairs. Jim Bowie was sick? Too sick to lead? She wondered if Juan knew.

Once outside, she watched the doctors stride to the long row of barracks used by the men. The day was overcast, the cloud cover offering a scant measure of warmth as she started once more across the yard. Men were digging a well in the open plaza. Others worked on the north wall, adding materials to reinforce it. She was glad to see some preparation finally taking place.

She paused for a moment to watch, noting the few men who stood around the workers, offering their advice but not helping with the manual labor. How could they be so lazy when Santa Anna was on his way?

Not at all like the broad-shouldered man in the midst of them who worked twice as hard as the others. He had removed his shirt, and the sweat gleamed across his back despite the chill in the air. The muscles in his arms and shoulders bulged as he raised a heavy log and positioned it, holding it while others lashed it together with the other beams for support. He called orders to the men, coordinating the entire process until he could step away from the log.

Realizing suddenly that she stared, she gripped the kettle and prepared to leave. With one more glance, she saw the man lean over, hands on his knees, and drag in several deep breaths. Straightening, he swiped the dark lock of hair from his eyes and she recognized Jake Dumont.

At that exact moment he noticed her. Slowly, without taking his gaze from her, he reached for a shovel that leaned against a mound of dirt. His face—so closely shaved the night before, now had the dark stubble of a new beard on his square jaw. She took a deep, rather unsteady breath at the vision he created—the dark hair sprinkled across his chest tapered to a line that disappeared into his buckskin pants.

Her eyes snapped back to his cool blue ones. He regarded her silently as heat suffused her face. She readjusted the kettle on her hip. She'd seen men work before and knew they were more comfortable at times without their shirts. So why did seeing his bare chest do crazy things to her insides—things that had never happened before? She clenched her hands around the iron rim. *Remember that he thinks only of himself,* she told herself. *You cannot trust him.*

The corded muscles of his arms flexed as he dropped his shovel and started toward her. "Señorita Torrez. We need to talk."

He stopped long enough to shrug into his shirt and slip on his hat before grasping her arm and leading her away from the others.

"Look at me that way again and everyone will know what you want." His voice was low in her ear, nearly a growl.

She jerked from his strong grip. "You flatter yourself, *señor.* I was amazed to find an Anglo like you without a burn. That is all."

"Right," he said dryly.

"Well, you are so careful to protect yourself from the discomfort of a bullet. I imagined you would feel the same way about the sun."

"Very funny—especially with it being winter. However, it's not the sun that is scorching me right now."

"Oh?" she said sweetly sarcastic.

"No. More the heat from your gaze."

Flustered at his words, she snapped her jaw shut. He truly was a beast of a man—uncouth and improper.

"I'm surprised you'd be thinking about me at all after I disappointed you last night," he continued in that smooth voice. "But it's nice to know you care."

"Do not twist my words."

"You're the one twisting mine—and a few other things, as well, I might add."

Oh, he really was a wicked man!

He glanced over her and she felt her cheeks flush. She hated that he could create such havoc inside her. It made her feel weak, and she knew she wasn't a weak person.

"What are you doing here…besides enjoying the view?"

"I came to collect my kettle, not that it is any of your concern." Her nose went up a notch.

He glanced inside the pot. "Any soup left?"

"Are you hungry or worried I might toss it at you?" she asked with sugary sweetness.

"Take your pick. Either way it would be worth it to have you look at me as you did a moment ago— preferably somewhere less crowded."

"Oh!" She sidestepped around him, having had enough. *"Buenos días, señor!"* She started across the plaza.

His low chuckle made her pause midstride even though she suspected he was baiting her with it. She turned back. What was he doing here? He didn't believe in the cause so why hadn't he left?

He waited, by his expression amused that she'd returned, but he did not tease her again.

"I am surprised to find you here…helping."

The planes of his face shifted and took on a certain hardness. "Don't think it's anything noble or that I've had a change of heart."

She shook her head quickly—too quickly, belying her words. "Of course not. How naive would that be?"

"My horse isn't ready for another long trip yet.

I'm just passing time—a day or two, until he heals up. Nothing more."

She indicated the men working at the wall. "You are not one to be idle, then."

"No. Never have been much of man of leisure. Doesn't suit me."

"I'm glad of it. There are too many lazy men about this fort. I'm glad to see you making things ready—preparing."

"Oh, I aim to please you, *señorita*. Just for today," he reminded her.

He was teasing her again, but it was different now—gentler, more amiable. This she could deal with easier than the tension-charged sparring she'd just endured. She let out a relieved sigh. "Just until your horse heals. I understand. Does the wound fester?"

He studied her, his deep blue eyes intent. "If you have a minute, I'll show you."

She hesitated. Such casual conversation with a man like him was new to her. Enticing, because he was so different than any man she'd ever met before—more rough, more reckless. Thrilling, too. Her parents, had they been present, would never allow such a conversation to take place. It would not have been proper.

His brow quirked up. "Looks like a war is going on between your ears, darlin'."

She frowned.

"What worries you?"

"It's not proper. Juan would not be pleased."

"Seguín?" He thought for a moment and she was gratified he didn't tease her again. "Understood. How about if we make sure to stay where we can be seen by others?"

She hesitated, but then nodded. "*Sí*. That would be acceptable."

He led her to the open horse corral adjacent to the church. The handful of horses plodding around the pen seemed as aimless as the soldiers who lounged outside. The large enclosure's adobe back wall doubled as the east wall of the fort and along it, a stall housed a large black stallion at least sixteen hands high. The horse stomped the dirt and whinnied as they approached, kicking up the odor of fresh straw and horse.

"Easy boy," Jake said soothingly. He ran the flat of his hand over the horse's neck and withers. An answering shudder vibrated through the beast as it quieted.

Victoria lowered her kettle to the ground and rubbed her arms. She was sure it was coincidence that she'd felt an awareness, too—as if his palm had been on her own skin. Disturbed, she shook the thought from her and stepped closer.

Jake stood near the horse, so that she had to move around him to check the gash on its hindquarters. She pressed the swelling at the stitches, noting the yellow drainage that oozed out. The horse stamped its hoof and snorted.

"Whoa, Fury."

"Here," she said, then moved her fingers lower on

the gash. "And here, the wound festers, but only slightly."

"Any suggestions?"

"Yes. A mixture of lard and kerosene to draw out the infection would help. I can make it up for you if you'd like."

She turned to get his reaction and suddenly noticed how close he was. A full head taller than she, he had successfully enclosed her between the wall and his horse, although, as he'd promised, her skirt could be seen by those lounging the perimeter of the corral. The horse's massive body blocked the rest of her from view. From here, the straight line of the Anglo's jaw was all she could see, that and the stubble of beard that coated it.

He kept his palm on his horse, calming it as he met her gaze. "You're not afraid of this big animal, are you?"

She smiled at such foolishness, tugging on the gold hoop earring in her ear. "I've been around horses all my life, *señor*. Why would I be afraid?"

He leaned closer, and the scent of musk and leather enveloped her.

She lowered her hand.

"You're not afraid of me, either." Under the brim of his hat, his eyes darkened. He raised his hand to stroke her cheek with fingers roughened but gentle. His touch left a trail of tingles behind.

Her breath hitched. "Should I be?"

He tilted her face toward his. "Definitely, *señorita*."

Her heart beat faster, caught as she was in his spell. "You cannot be trusted to act the gentleman?"

He focused on her lips, his intent now obvious. "Never learned how."

A lump formed in her throat. He wanted to kiss her. She swallowed hard. It wasn't proper. She should resist, but she was curious. His lips, set there in the middle of his dark day-old beard looked impossibly soft for someone so tough. How would they feel against hers? How would he taste?

He lowered his mouth to hers. Warmth rushed from his lips to hers, sending heat through her body. Not unpleasant at all, she thought, adjusting her lips slightly to his mouth. He slid his hand around the back of her neck and pulled her closer, his mouth firm against hers now, moving, opening…

Her heart raced. The only time she'd been kissed before, she'd been sixteen. Esteban's fumbling kiss was child's play compared to this man's kiss. This was not a sweet request for a mutual sampling, but a demand, hard and full of need. Passion penetrated it—daring her to satisfy her curiosity at her own risk.

Even though continuing might place her teetering on the brink of peril, she was not ready to stop yet. Tentatively she relaxed her lips, allowing his tongue to touch hers. Fire rushed to her center, searing her, melting her resistance. Perhaps this was a mistake after all. Perhaps this was more than she could handle. Suddenly her knees weakened and buckled.

He broke off the kiss and caught her, supporting

her effortlessly. He set her from him and stared at her, confusion clouding his face.

Stunned at the intensity of his kiss, she forced herself to straighten, finding her legs beneath her still unsteady. Heat flamed in her cheeks. She covered them with her hands. That had been more than she'd expected.

Without a word, she edged around him and started across the corral.

"Señorita."

She heard his call, but kept going at a brisk clip. She had to get away from him. Had to think clearly again. He was dangerous. More than she'd ever imagined.

"Victoria!"

Oh, this wouldn't do—calling after her like a common *soldadera.* Anyone could hear. Juan could hear. She dragged in a great gulp of cold air and turned to give him a scathing retort.

He held up the kettle. "You forgot this." As she reached for it, he pulled it close to himself. "I'll carry it. It's the least I can do if you're going to help my horse."

Thank goodness he did not mention the kiss. Her emotions whirled around her in chaotic images, embarrassment foremost in her mind. "I can manage."

"I'm not saying you can't."

He wasn't teasing her any longer. His eyes were serious. Her breathing finally slowed to normal. "Thank you."

He walked beside her as they left the fort and

crossed the footbridge over the San Antonio River. She barely noticed the two little boys throwing stones into the water as she hurried across the wooden planks.

"Victoria…about what just happened," he began.

She swallowed hard and looked straight ahead. "I am sorry for it, Señor Dumont. Please do not recall it."

"It's nothing to be upset about."

"You do not understand." Part of her was embarrassed, but another part deeper inside was thrilled and that made her all the more dismayed at herself. How could her body betray her like that? "You do not understand," she repeated.

He put a hand on her arm, gently slowing her steps. "Explain it to me then."

Now he was kind. What was it about this man that called to her so? "I can't. It…it isn't you. I'm angry with myself. What I did would mortify my parents. How could I let you touch me? You're—you're not even Catholic!"

He pulled her to a stop. "Now wait a minute. I think I had a little influence on what just happened, too. Don't shoulder the whole thing like some martyr. And, Victoria, it was just a kiss!"

It was far more than a kiss to her. If he wasn't affected by it, it just proved how innocent she was and how foolish. Exasperation with him and with herself lent anger to her words. "Oh! You…you… *hombre!*"

His gaze narrowed.

She was getting worked up to a fine temper but couldn't seem to stop. "There is nothing nice about you! Do not talk to me anymore. And give me back my kettle." She faced him and, grabbing hold of the large pot, she tugged it toward herself.

He kept hold of the rim.

The glare she gave him should have burned him to a crisp. He was just too mean to disintegrate into smoke. When she tugged on the pot again, he finally let go.

"Strange," he said, staring down the street. "Seems awful quiet today. Wonder what's going on?"

She followed his gaze and for the first time noticed that the gun shop was closed and the milliner's, too. "Perhaps Lieutenant Colonel Travis has allowed some of the men leave to check on their homes. Juan said he was going to request it first thing this morning."

"Maybe," he said, but he didn't sound convinced and still scrutinized the side streets and yards.

Victoria cleared her throat, drawing back his attention. "I can make it the rest of the way myself," she said with as much dignity as she could muster.

He stepped back and tipped the brim of his hat. "I'll just say good day then, Señorita Torrez. And thank you."

Conscious that he watched her, she strode down the street, not slowing her pace until she reached Juan's doorstep. Before she stepped through the portal, she couldn't help glancing back at him. He'd already turned and headed back to the fort.

"Good," she murmured to herself although she remained irritated at him. She had important things to consider, and his presence made it difficult to think rationally.

However, once she entered the parlor she couldn't think of anything but his kiss. The caress had been important to her and it hurt to know Señor Dumont hadn't been as taken with her as she was with him— even if curiosity had been her initial reason for kissing him. She touched her lips, wondering that she could still feel the insistent press of his mouth against hers. They had been soft…and smooth. Oh, so smooth. Her hands clenched. The *hombre!*

She walked into the kitchen and let out a shriek.

Chapter Five

Esteban stood in the middle of the kitchen, his chest heaving as he sucked in air to breathe. Sweat rolled down his forehead and dampened and curled his black hair. His uniform clung to him.

Recovering from her initial reaction of fright, she ran to him. "Esteban! What are you doing here?" she whispered frantically. "Is it my parents? Do you have word of them?"

"They are gone."

"No!" she cried. "No! I should have been there with them."

Esteban shook her gently by the shoulders. "Victoria! Quiet yourself. They ran off in the night. The army searched for a day and found no trace of them. Food was missing, and horses from the corral, so I know they slipped away. And Santa Anna did not want to search longer for one old man and woman."

"My parents are not old!" she said indignantly.

"The officers were not overworried at their disappearance."

Calculating the days since she'd last seen Esteban, she paused. "You did not have time to return all the way to Laredo since I last saw you. How do you know this?"

Esteban hesitated slightly. "From my second in command. He sent word."

She breathed a sigh of relief. "They will return when it is safe to do so, just as I hope to. I have to believe that." She looked over his blue uniform. "You aren't safe here dressed like that. Let me find something of Juan's for you to wear."

"No. Victoria—wait. There isn't time." The urgency in his voice had her turning back to him from the doorway. "You cannot stay here. You must leave immediately and get to safety."

"Is it Santa Anna? Is he near?"

He nodded. "A few miles out. I raced to get here."

The church bell started clanging, startling them both. Victoria felt Esteban's grip tighten on her shoulders, almost hurtful before releasing her. In the streets, men shouted to each other. She glanced out the window. A woman with a baby wrapped in her arms was hurrying toward the fort. A young child, clinging to her skirt, slowed her progress.

Her chest tightened. "It has finally happened, then. All that we have feared."

"There was never a doubt."

"Oh, Esteban! You take such a risk coming here to warn me."

"I will get back before anyone knows I am missing. It's you I'm concerned about." He glanced about the room. "Quick. Gather your things. Come with me."

The determination in his voice frightened her. "But I must go to the fort with the others!"

He pressed his lips together. "No. Victoria... please come with me. I'll protect you."

She shook her head. "You should go back now," she said firmly. At his worried expression, she threw her arms about his neck. "I will be fine. You are dear to me, Esteban. Stay safe."

The front door slammed open and heavy footsteps sounded on the wooden floor of the parlor. "Señorita Torrez! Victoria!"

She recognized Jake's voice seconds before he appeared at the kitchen doorway.

"You need to—" He stopped abruptly when he spotted her with Esteban.

Jake's eyes narrowed, his gaze running down the length of the soldier's uniform. "What the hell is going on?"

Esteban stepped forward, his manner commanding, his hand on the hilt of his sword. "Who is this, Victoria? What is he doing here?"

She put a hand to his chest to stop him. "No, *por favor.*"

She turned to Jake, but for her life could not think what to say to explain a soldier's presence in the house.

"I asked first, if I recall," Jake said. He studied her

critically. "Was all that talk last night about your land and independence a lie?"

She gasped. That he would think such a thing angered her. She was no traitor. "I cannot explain right now, Señor Dumont. Please, you must go."

"Perhaps he should be the one to leave," Jake said with a calmness that did little to cover the steel edge to his voice. "His army is just over the rise."

The Anglo had no fear—no fear at all! But then, he did not comprehend the situation here.

"He is my good friend," she said, letting her anger show. "And you are not welcome here any longer."

Jake stepped back as if she'd slapped him. His gaze turned cold. "You've got two minutes, then I'm taking you to the fort whether you have your things packed or not. No arguments." He spun on his heel and left the room.

"He will make trouble for you," Esteban said, disapproval in his voice.

Victoria's heart pounded. Trouble? Everywhere that man went he made trouble. She looked up at Esteban. "No. I think not. He does not want to get involved with our fight. He will leave town now."

Esteban searched her face for a moment as if questioning whether to believe her or go after Jake. Coming to a decision, he stepped into the hall and quickly checked the other rooms of the house. "Where is Seguín? Why are you with this Anglo instead of him?"

Before she could answer, he continued. "You should come with me. You are not being protected properly." He took her arm.

She tried to twist from his grip. "No! I cannot!"

Esteban's gaze hardened on hers.

"I will not!" She braced herself.

The bell in the church tower rang out again, louder this time.

Indecision crossed his face for a moment, and then he released her. "All right, Victoria. I wish to spare you from the bloodshed, but you will have your own way I see. Hear this—when the battle is over, then you will come with me. You will have no other choice if you wish to survive."

As quickly and silently as he had entered the house, he left, moving down the back alley as stealthily as a panther.

Jake paced at the front entrance to Juan's house watching the melee in the street, although his thoughts centered on Victoria and the soldier with her, trying to make sense of what he'd just seen.

Men, women and children, their arms loaded with blankets, pillows and food, loaded everything into carts or slung makeshift packs on their backs and headed to the fort. A man in the bell tower pointed to the south and yelled to some men in the street, his words drowned out by the constant ringing of the bells.

"Santa Anna! He is here!" a boy cried out, tugging at his younger sister and hurrying her along. Another girl of about twelve years herded chickens, squawking and clucking, toward the bridge. Three boys half a block away pulled on a stubborn cow.

Although they yelled insults in English and in Spanish, the animal bawled and locked her legs against their tugging. Jake ran across the street and gave the bovine a mighty slap on its bony hip, startling it so that it took off at an awkward gait.

He didn't want to believe Victoria was conspiring with the enemy—not after all her noble words. But the vision of her with her arms around the soldier haunted him. It wasn't as though the man was trying to hide anything—not with him wearing that peacock of a uniform. He could be using subterfuge to wrest information out of her without her realizing it, information about Juan and Travis, about their plans, and then going right back to Santa Anna with it. Jake didn't want to believe she was that gullible.

Enough. It wasn't like him to turn his back on what had happened inside the house. He'd waited too long as it was for Señorita Torrez. The minute the bells had sounded the alarm, he'd taken off at a run, worried that she had come to harm. And this was the thanks he got. She'd kicked him out!

He stormed back inside. *"Señorita!"* he boomed. "We are going now!"

Victoria appeared in a doorway off the great hall, slipping her dark blue cloak around her shoulders. She didn't meet his gaze, instead she kept her eye on her things—two large woven baskets, nearly as big as herself, filled to overflowing with household items.

"Are you ready?"

She brought her dark eyes up to stare into his. *"Sí, señor. I am ready."*

He'd worry later about the anger smoldering just beneath the surface of her gaze. Right now he had to get her safely to the fort. He slung one basket over his back and gripped a handle on the other lighter one. She gripped the opposite handle and together they lifted it between them. Leading the way, he stepped out into the street.

A commotion grew behind them. Men yelled and a woman screamed. Was it the soldiers? He turned and caught sight of a sorrel horse charging down the street, snorting and kicking at anything in its way. A dog sped out from one of the houses and began barking incessantly at the beast, which then careened toward them.

Jake dropped the baskets and ran toward the horse, waving his arms. At the last minute, he gave a shrill whistle and the animal veered off toward a side street, kicking up large clods. Dirt and stones pelted them. Victoria dropped the basket and shielded her face as her goods spewed all over the street.

Turning to her, he searched for cuts or scratches on her perfect skin. "Are you injured?"

She shook her head.

He helped her to stand, only to realize she was unsteady. Swaying, she put her hand to her forehead.

"Dammit, you could have been killed!"

Her eyes clouded over at his coarse words, but she had the presence to frown at him. A small thing, but he was grateful, for it meant she wasn't seriously hurt.

Slowly, gingerly, she began picking up the scattered items. "I'm fine."

As he helped load the baskets, Jake only half noted the fine quality of the blankets and the abundance of canned goods and expensive beeswax candles rather than tallow.

Unable again to put the matter of the Mexican soldier behind him, he asked. "Who was that man?" He made it clear with the tone of his voice that there would be no hedging now.

"I told you. A good friend." Yet she still wouldn't look him in the eye.

"But not a patriot. Not a Texian."

"No."

"I'd like to know which side he's really on, that's all. And by association…you."

Her mouth opened wide in shocked surprise and then in a huff she wrenched her arm free of his grip. "You don't know me at all, Señor Dumont, if you think I'd hurt Juan by associating with the enemy."

"But you are."

She bit her lower lip, and he could tell she was trying to figure out how much to tell him. "How do you know he isn't a spy for us?"

He wanted to believe her. There were just too many things that pointed to her being tricked by the man. He shook his head in disgust. "Deny it now, Victoria, and I still won't believe you."

In silence they crossed the bridge and entered the mission/fort with the others. He followed her, along with the other women and children, to the sacristy of the church.

In the small area, several pallets lined the walls.

Women worked at building beds of hay in the center of the room. Jake walked over to one of these and dropped her things. He eyed it with disdain. A bit of a change for her. Obviously she was used to nicer things—at least a real bed. Good thing it wasn't his problem.

She smoothed a loose tendril of hair off her cheek and tucked it within her bun. "Thank you for your help. I'll find Juan and let him know I am here."

He nodded, knowing that would be best. "I'll leave you then. Goodbye, *señorita*."

"Wait." She plucked a jar from atop her satchel and handed it to him.

"What's this?"

"Liniment. For your horse."

He stared at the jar before tossing it back in the basket. "Before this is over, the men here will need it more than my horse does."

"I don't think so," she said quietly. "Juan says Santa Anna does not take prisoners."

The thought sobered him all the more.

She straightened her spine. "Thank you for your help, Señor Du—Jake."

It was not lost on him that she'd finally used his given name.

"I wish you success in finding your brother," she said. "Go now, before there is no way out."

He looked once more at her standing beside her pallet with her two baskets and knew she was right. If he was going to find Brandon, he had to be about it. "Goodbye, Victoria."

He caught the scent of her perfumed soap, so incongruent with the smell of straw and stone in the room. Barely comprehending what he was doing, he memorized the smell before leaving her.

Outside, the men were charged with an intensity and energy that had been missing previously—no doubt due to the realization that the rumors were now inevitably true. Santa Anna and his army would soon be here and the Texians had to be ready.

The thought of Victoria in the middle of such a battle made his gut clench. It was obvious she was from money, and even though she didn't act as one who had been coddled all her life, she still didn't have the slightest clue what could happen to her when men were worked into a blood frenzy. He'd like to shake some sense into her. Land wasn't worth the risk she was taking.

Seguín stood near the east wall, issuing orders to several men, but looked at him as Jake passed. The Tejano's nod was almost imperceptible. Jake recognized it for what it was—an understanding, in a way a permission, to leave. He gripped his rifle tighter. Seguín would take care of Victoria now. Let him worry about the soldier in the house—if Victoria chose to tell him. She wasn't Jake's concern any longer.

So why did he feel this way? Like a two-headed snake pulling in opposite directions?

Too bad he couldn't stay. He'd like nothing better than to peel back her layers…figuratively… Well, maybe literally, too, he decided, thinking of the way her soft warm body had swayed to the music in the cantina and how she'd felt when he'd kissed her. He would never admit it to her but that kiss had stunned him. Up until then she had been an intriguing interlude from which he could easily walk away. But when he'd caught a glimpse of the passionate woman waiting inside, things had definitely changed.

Leaving was the smart thing to do—*before* doing something crazy like sampling more than a simple kiss.

When he entered the corral, Fury greeted him with a toss of his dark head and a snort. Considering the commotion in the yard outside, it didn't surprise him that his horse knew something was afoot. Murmuring quiet words to calm him, Jake slid his hand over the beast's withers. Fury sidestepped and flicked his tail. He saddled the horse, lashed on his bedroll and gave the horse a chance to drink from the trough before he mounted. Taking a last look around, his gaze fixed for a moment on the church where Victoria stayed. Then he urged Fury out of the corral and toward the Alamo gates.

He rode through the gate, wondering if he only imagined the sudden drop in temperature on the outside wall of the mission/fort. Men, women and children headed toward him and crowded through the opening, their faces full of anxiety and fear and something else—resolve. Jake knew that feeling. He'd felt it when he set off after Brandon. He felt it growing inside of him now.

Chapter Six

At noon, Santa Anna's army paraded unchallenged down the main street of Béxar toward the Alamo mission compound and secured the town. As Victoria crouched next to Diego on the wide stone wall of the mission by the main gate, she saw a few brave souls, loyal to the general, peeking out from the doorways of their homes. Two young boys hid behind barrels in a side street. Victoria could see them plainly enough from her vantage point. They stared, wide-eyed toward the other end of the street, hoping to catch a glimpse of the general up close.

The regimental band was the first to appear, playing lively music and escorted by men carrying flags and banners of Mexico. A line of soldiers, at least one hundred strong, followed and fanned out in two rows in the town square. From this distance their uniforms of blue trousers and red coats, with brass buttons shining in the winter sun, appeared elegant and smart compared to the ragtag buckskin and homespun wool of the Texian army. Their muskets, fixed with bayonets and held close to their side, were perfectly aligned and spaced throughout the square.

Behind this first contingent rode the officers on horseback. Although she tried, Victoria could not make out Esteban from this distance and couldn't be sure he was there. Santa Anna came next, sitting astride his horse tall and silent, his feathered hat blowing in the light breeze. The weak sunlight glinted off his golden sword handle.

"Look at him," Diego said, awed. "I have never seen anything like it. He enters like a king with his court."

"He believes he is one," Victoria said, unable to keep the worry from her voice. Everything about the man frightened her—his small black eyes, his perfectly coiffed hair, his too-clean uniform. "But he is just a man."

Diego snorted next to her. "You are difficult to impress."

"He does this to scare us. To show us he is not afraid."

"It's working. Look how many there are."

As far down the street as she could strain to see there were soldiers marching. The officers rode horses along with one regiment of dragoons, but the rest were mostly foot soldiers, carrying their lances and muskets smartly at their sides.

Juan moved beside her to watch, his face grim. "They just keep coming and coming."

Diego nodded and fell silent.

Santa Anna stopped at the main square, but his men kept pouring into the area. They continued to fan out away from his horse and the other officers, keeping a set distance as would befit a king surrounded by his underlings, marching to the drummer's beat. Finally the order to halt was given and they stopped, standing ramrod straight, looking neither left nor right. The effect was dazzling—and frightening.

Unable to take her eyes from the display before her, Victoria's thoughts wandered to what could have happened had she not met Señor Dumont. What if she had been unable to bring her things to the fort? What if Señor Dumont hadn't been there to help her? She made the sign of the cross over her breast. Surely God was looking out for her and had used him as her protector.

She said a quick prayer for his safe journey. The irony of her praying for him caught at her. He thought her a willing confidant to Esteban. She'd seen it in his eyes, in the way he'd looked at her when he said in his deep voice, "Deny it, and I still won't believe you."

She closed her eyes to the brightly colored plaza. She would never forget the kiss. At once embarrassed and yet also amazed at the depth of feeling it evoked in her, she knew Señor Dumont may have ruined her for any other man. Now she would yearn for such a deep, passionate kiss from the man she would marry. A man of Spanish descent, of course.

She opened her eyes and gave herself a mental shake. The Anglo was gone. It would be best to forget him. Thank God Juan had not learned of her display at the corral.

A movement at the town's church caught her eye. While everyone watched, a soldier gained quick access to the top of the bell tower and lowered the tricolored flag the Texians had flying. He wadded it into a messy ball and threw it to the dirt below. Then two men hoisted a blood-red flag over the square. General Santa Anna eyed the flag and then with an imperious tilt to his chin looked across the river at the Alamo in a direct challenge. He now had control of the town.

"What does the flag mean, Juan?" Victoria asked.

Juan glanced at Diego and then met her gaze. "No quarter will be given. No prisoners will be taken."

So it was true. Worry twisted inside as Victoria looked over the compound. The only sound she heard was the cold wind rustling the leaves on the cottonwoods nearby. The soldiers behind the walls of the Alamo had grown silent with Santa Anna's display. The situation they'd bullied about and discussed constantly over the past weeks had become more than a threat. Now it was real.

The Mexicans fired a cannon and the shell landed short of the fort. Victoria gasped and backed away from the edge. It had begun! From the Texians a volley of rifle shots sounded and then the report of the eighteen pounder reverberated. The cannon shell sailed through the air over the town and exploded beyond the last house, an answer to Santa Anna rather than a counterattack.

"We need more men," Juan said without taking his eyes off the Mexican army.

"They will come," she murmured fervently, hoping against hope that she was right. "They must come."

"Let us hope so. For now, you shouldn't be up here on the roof. This is no place for a lady," he said.

She frowned. "But I don't want to be tucked out of the way. I want to help."

"And you will. Just not on the roof with the men. I want you to stay with the other women for now." Keeping low, he helped her crawl back from the wall and climb down the ladder near the main gate—not an easy task in her skirt.

Juan glanced about the fort's perimeter, counting off the number of soldiers on the walls. "It is a small thing, but good, that your Anglo friend decided to lend a hand."

Her breath caught. Jake? Here? "No. You are mistaken, Juan. He left this morning right after he helped me to the fort." Still, she looked around at the men on the wall, searching for his black hat.

"He brought in a wagon load of corn from the *jacales* earlier and then helped some men round up the cattle and drive them inside the fort." Juan jutted his chin toward the south wall, but watched her closely. "He's on the wall. Standing beside the cannon."

She scanned the area until she found him leaning

against the iron weapon. He hadn't left after all! She stared at him in wonderment. Had he suddenly been convinced of the need to fight? Why had he changed his mind?

Diego stepped away from the wall and joined them. "You say he helped you to the fort?"

She nodded, hearing the speculation in his young voice.

"Instead of leaving?"

"Yes." Exasperation quickly worked its way to the surface. She didn't like that look on his face. "I don't know why, he just did. But I'm glad. Otherwise I would have been trampled by a runaway horse."

Juan rubbed his chin. "And now he stays. He checked in with Travis an hour ago."

"Jake signed up?" It was hard to believe after all his talk.

"It's Jake now?" Juan said as he studied her face. Then he shook his head. "He didn't commit to anything, didn't sign anything, just offered to help."

"That sounds like him," she said. "The only thing he is committed to is himself—and possibly his brother."

"Maybe," Juan said, continuing to study her.

"Don't let him fool you. Not this man," Victoria said, hands on hips. "You can be sure I'll be very careful around him."

"Good. Remember always that he is Americano. Not like us. But also remember that a man's actions say more about him than what comes out of his mouth. You would do well to remember that."

Frustrated that Juan didn't wholeheartedly side with her, Victoria looked once more at the men on the walls. A chill went through her. She had counted over one thousand soldiers in the square and they kept coming. The odds that the small battalion inside the Alamo would survive were tiny unless help came.

Although unable to see Jake's face from this angle, she could tell by his tense stance and the clenched hands that he was ready for whatever should come. Why had he stayed? He'd said clearly that he didn't believe their fight was worth it. And now, because of Esteban, Jake thought she was a traitor. None of it made any sense to her. Still, watching him now, she felt her heart squeeze again in her chest.

Jake was stunned. Seeing the magnitude of Santa Anna's army shattered any illusion he had that changing his mind and leaving would be possible. The first volley of shots ended and again the bugles sounded. Travis was nowhere to be seen when suddenly the gates opened slightly and someone on a horse rode out through them carrying a white flag of truce toward the town.

A parlay? And who had called it?

Whether or not it worked, Jake didn't believe the time should be wasted. Although the sun was close to setting, Santa Anna would not rest and neither would he. He strode down the dirt ramp toward Travis's office to get orders. Before he walked through the door he heard the lieutenant colonel's voice. "I won't negotiate with a madman! How dare Bowie go behind my back!"

Jake backed out of Travis's office. Two leaders calling different courses of action? Not a good omen. He headed toward the north wall. Enough of the day was left to put in a good hour or two on the weakest point of the fort.

Most of the men there were as shocked as he was, nerves stretched thin under the sudden increase of stress.

"What the hell are we doing here?" mumbled a large German as he forced mud into the cracks around the logs.

"You heard the rumors as much as the rest of us. You had time to leave," grumbled another older man.

Jake recognized him as the fiddler in the cantina the night of the fandango. "Why didn't you go when you had the chance?" Jake asked him.

Without a moment of hesitation, the fiddler spit in the dirt and then answered. "I got land here. Never had land before in my life. I aim to keep it."

"And it's worth dying for?" Jake asked, unable to keep the edge of sarcasm from his voice.

The man stared at him—hard. "Yep." Then he turned back to shoveling dirt, his movements purposeful and determined. He looked to be in his forties, Jake thought, with his lamb-chop sideburns graying before the rest of his sandy-red hair. By the steady pace he established, he was no stranger to work.

The rest of the men had quieted at his question,

each in their own way pondering it again. Yet none of them stopped working, none of them eased off. If anything, they increased their activity with renewed fervor.

Feeling the odd man out, Jake joined them again, packing an old rag into the cracks between two beams and earned a gruff nod from the man he'd questioned. Picking up an ax he started trimming the branches off a small log. Something was happening here he didn't understand. It was palpable. He could feel it infusing all of them with a sense of purpose.

Why had he stayed? Even he didn't understand why. At the time, riding Fury away had been harder than riding back toward the Alamo gates, so he'd turned around.

His father would have laughed, Jake realized, his gut clenching at the thought. He would have expected him to do something dumb like this—to get pulled off course in the middle of searching for Brandon. The man was right. What was Jake thinking to let a woman make him question his decision and cloud his reason? Hadn't he learned his lesson long ago that loyalty was an illusion? An impossible dream—empty and crippling?

Land had no such ability. It was only grass, rocks, dirt—not alive and breathing. Men were fools to lust after it, to want to own it and subdue it to their purposes, expecting in return that the land would give back to them a measure of the blood and sweat that had been put into it. That they'd gain wealth or power from it.

Women, on the other hand, may desire loyalty, may demand loyalty, but were incapable of returning it. Like the woman who had given him birth—his mother.

It didn't matter whether it was to land or to a woman, Jake wouldn't give that part of himself to anyone, nor would he expect it in return. Señorita Torrez was right in one thing—he was loyal only to himself.

He rammed his ax into the log with such force that he felt it vibrate throughout his body. Straightening, he stretched out the tightness in his lower back.

Perhaps he should thank Victoria for bringing him back to reality. He'd do best to look out for himself.

The sun had set hours ago by the time Jake finished watering Fury in the horse compound and began to consider sleep. He was dog tired and the straw filled mattress he'd staked out in the barracks held an appeal better than the open ground he'd slept on while traveling into Texian territory. At the moment he was hungry and cold—in that order.

He stepped from the corral and breathed in a lungful of the mesquite-smoke-filled air. His mouth watered. Somewhere, food was being prepared and he aimed to get some. Maybe he'd just walk by the church where the women were staying or see if there was a kitchen.

On the way, he ran into Juan and Diego. "Been looking for you, Anglo," Juan said. "Come with us."

He followed, telling himself it was in the hopes of catching a good meal rather than the desire to see Victoria again.

She sat on a log by a small campfire, tending to a pot from which steam rose into the night air. She tucked her dark-green skirt around her ankles as he neared but didn't look up at him.

"Look who we found," Diego said with a grin.

She had to look up then, or risk being rude. "Hello, Señor Dumont. You are welcome to have something to eat with us. It is not much, but it will fill you."

So formal. It set him back for a moment, but then he realized it must be because of Juan and Diego watching closely. If that's how she wanted to play it, fine by him. He touched his hat. "Thank you, ma'am. I'd like that."

Her gaze flickered up at his use of *ma'am*.

He upended a small barrel and sat across the fire from her where he could enjoy the view and try to make some sense of what he thought of her. Warm firelight flickered over her face, enhancing the contours and angles and flushing her cheeks as she worked. The small gold hoops in her ears shimmered. Her thick dark hair had fallen from its knot and lay curled down her back. Not so proper now. He liked her this way—softer. A strand of hair fell forward over her cheek. She brushed it aside with the back of her hand and leaned over to stir the pot, her cream-colored blouse gaping slightly. Settled above the rise of her breasts shimmered a small golden crucifix.

She poured the cooked cereal into a carved gourd and moved around the fire to hand it to him. Briefly their fingers touched as he took the bowl. A quick glance and then she returned to her seat and dished up food for Juan.

"You're not having any?" Jake asked.

"In a moment. When you are finished with the bowl."

Dutifully he took a spoonful of the mush. It was sweet, filling. "What is this?"

"*Atole*—ground and boiled corn."

He took another bite.

"It came from the wagon you brought in," Juan said. "We won't starve now. Not with the cattle and the corn. And we have plenty of water." He finished his *atole* and handed the gourd to Diego, who quickly refilled it and ate with the gusto of a growing boy.

Realizing he was taking his time and Victoria might be hungry, Jake hurried with his food. He rose and handed the empty bowl back to her. "Thank you."

She nodded and helped herself.

Juan stood and stretched his legs. "I need to speak with Travis. Diego? Let my men know I'll be over to see them afterward."

Diego grunted his acknowledgment and went back to eating. When he was done, he rose and set the bowl down by the fire. "Not Maria's, but not bad," he said with a grin, earning him a glare.

And suddenly Jake was alone with her. If being in the middle of 150 or so men, enclosed in a fort could be called "alone." He watched as she cleaned up the bowls, noticing her slender fingers and wrists. Her shawl slipped from her shoulder, the end dragging in the dirt.

He stood and stepped toward her, taking the end of the cloth and adjusting it on her. Still she would not meet his gaze.

"Gracías," she said quietly, going back to her work. And shutting him out.

She didn't seem to want any part of him. Or care that he'd decided to stay. Frustrated with himself for letting her get to him, he grabbed her arm and pulled her to her feet.

"Why are you acting like this?" he demanded. "You run hot and cold."

"Señor Du—"

"Don't *Señor* me, Victoria. It was Jake before— when you thought I was leaving."

Her eyes flashed in the firelight.

Good. He'd struck a nerve. He let go of her arm.

Immediately she stepped away from him to the other side of the fire pit. "What are you doing here, Jake? Why didn't you leave?"

He ran a hand through his hair. "Good question. Guess I thought I'd get a thank-you out of it."

She met his gaze with a warning look. "If you think you will get another kiss out of this, don't worry. I learned my lesson. My curiosity is satisfied, and I will not be so foolish again."

"Is that what it was all about? Your curiosity? And here I thought you liked me by the way you were looking at me in the plaza."

"It was no more than the way you looked at me in the stable. You, too, wanted a taste. Or was it all about the conquest?"

"I didn't force you to do anything you weren't wanting," he said, pretty sure she had him pegged and hating it. "Why would I want a kiss from a woman who meets with the enemy?"

"If you knew me, you would not make such accusations," she said, banked anger simmering in her voice.

"If you knew me, you would know why I stayed."

She held up her finger. "Don't you dare put this on my shoulders. I do know you. You are not so noble that you would do this for the same reasons that I am. You are only interested in yourself."

"So now a man can only fight if his reasons are as pure as yours? Is that it?" he asked, incredulous. "I thought you were willing to take anybody."

Hands on hips she glared at him.

"It is all black-and-white to you, isn't it, Victoria? Either I am gung ho on the fight for freedom or I'm a bad person because I don't think the same way that you do. Well, let me enlighten you. There are all shades of gray in this world, and you better get used to seeing them now that you are off your ranch and out in the big world."

That earned him a very unladylike snort.

She stared at him over the flames, and all he could think about was the kiss they'd shared and how it had consumed him—how he wanted another whether she was a spy or not. He'd take his chances. She had bewitched him, he realized. It was as if that rattler had curled up inside him and was waiting… waiting…its tail vibrating. He moved closer.

The look on her face suddenly changed, grew wary. "Jake…"

He stopped midstep on his way to her.

"There is no way that you can kiss me again. I cannot allow it. I am bound by my place in life, my birthright, as much as you are not bound."

"Don't flatter yourself too much there, princess," he said. "Who says I've got that on my mind? As kisses go, you held your own, but that doesn't mean I can't live without another one."

Her jaw dropped open.

He hadn't meant to snarl. She'd probably never had anyone talk to her like that before. He'd let his anger get the better of him and here she'd gone to the trouble to make enough food for him. If he didn't shut up soon, he'd end up regretting a whole passel of things. Still, he couldn't quite get past the fact she thought he was inferior.

"You are right about one thing. I don't have a blood-line going back centuries, however the family I do have is respected in Charleston." Even as he said the words, he knew they were mostly a lie. Brandon was respected in Charleston, not him. His brother was the only family Jake had left—and he was somewhere here in Texas territory trying to get as far away from Jake as possible. The thought sobered him. Enough was enough. He didn't need to stay and endure her condescension.

"Thank you for the meal, *Señorita*."

"You are welcome," she said, the words clipped and short.

He tipped his hat and headed for the barracks. Hopefully the snores of the men would drown out his foolish thoughts and he could sleep.

Chapter Seven

The loud blast of a cannon startled Victoria awake. She rose on one elbow, looking around the room. For most of the night she had tossed and turned, kept awake by the exchange of gunfire and the children's whimpers. She tried to make sense of her surroundings, surprised that she'd fallen asleep so soundly in the early hours of the morning.

It had not helped that in her sleep-filled mind she continually played out her last encounter with Jake. It shouldn't matter what he thought about her, but it did. It hurt that he didn't trust her. She'd been so upset at dinner their first evening at the fort that she'd said nothing to defend herself and then yesterday she'd not seen him at all.

But you shouldn't have to defend yourself! A small voice inside told her. *He should believe you.*

The truth of the matter was that they had no claim on each other and what he did and thought shouldn't affect her so. What she had said was true. There could never be anything between them because of their stations in life. Her family would never accept him. He was a drifter with nothing to show for himself but a beautiful stallion. Her parents would expect her to marry well—for land or title. And if by some chance she did not see her mother or father again, she would honor the trust they placed in her.

She mustn't let him upset her. All of her attention should be focused on how to help in this battle. The comings and goings of one man should not engulf her mind as it was doing.

Nearby a baby wailed. His mother clucked soothingly and cuddled him closer even as the baby resisted comforting. The young woman looked frightened herself. Victoria wondered if she was a wife to one of the soldiers. The woman unbuttoned her blouse and offered her breast for the baby to suckle. As the babe latched on greedily, a warm fluttering stirred in Victoria's stomach. Fascinated by the sight of the small fist curled against its mother's breast and the contented sighs and slurps coming from the baby, Victoria watched, while throughout the room, children and women began stirring.

Throwing off the cloak that she'd used for a blanket through the night, Victoria stood and tucked her blouse back into her skirt's waist. Then she finger combed her hair, plaited it, and hooked it atop her head as best she could before stepping outside.

The sun sat on the horizon, casting a purple-pink glow in the east. Men ran across the dirt plaza, calling out to their fellow comrades as they relieved the men on duty and positioned themselves for watching the Mexican army. In the southwest corner, soldiers angled the largest cannon, an eighteen-pounder Juan had said, into a better position to damage the enemy.

She looked about for Juan and Diego. They'd want coffee soon enough. She headed for the fort's kitchen.

Several women prepared and served breakfast, bustling about the large room while the soldiers ate. Victoria threw coffee grounds into a tall pot, filled it with water from a nearby jug and placed it on the fire grate. Then she poured cornmeal into a large wooden bowl and added water. As she worked the dough to make tortillas she found herself searching among the men for Jake. When there was no sign of him, she berated herself that she'd even looked. What would they have to say to each other, anyway?

She must think about what she could do to help. Perhaps there was a need at the hospital for some of her poultices or good, hearty soup. Anything to keep her mind off Jake and the questions that swirled in her head every time she thought of him.

"*Buenos días,* Victoria."

Victoria looked up to see Juan standing before her. His shoulders slumped in fatigue as he removed his hat.

"Did you just come from standing watch?" she asked, noting the dark circles under his eyes.

"No, but it was a restless night nonetheless. You were deep in thought just now. You are thinking of home?"

She smiled wanly. "No. Of many things, but not of home."

"The Anglo?"

She tilted her head and said too quickly. "No—about what I will do today to help."

Juan slid onto a bench at the long table. She set a tin cup in front of him and did the same for Diego as he joined them.

"What of your meeting last night?" she asked, wanting to get the focus off Jake.

"Travis wants the well finished as soon as possible. And we must make the north wall stronger. It is still our weakest point."

"So you will keep busy today."

Juan nodded. "He also wants the cannon fired three times a day, to let those in the country know that we continue to hold the fort. Otherwise, we must conserve our ammunition."

"The sound woke me this morning."

"I am glad you could sleep at all." He reached for a warm buttered tortilla and ate it in four bites.

The coffee hot, she poured his cup first and then Diego's. Seared beefsteaks—cooked by a woman in front of the fire, were served up next.

"Thank you. I mean no offense to your cooking skills, but perhaps tonight I will have Maria bring something from the house."

Victoria glanced up sharply. "You are able to do that?"

"Diego can get word to her. And then we may learn something more about our enemy."

"Or he may learn more about you," she said, thinking how easy it had been for Jake to think of her as a conspirator. Perhaps there was reason for him to question a Tejano's allegiance. Perhaps others were communicating outside the fort, too. "Be careful, Juan. I don't like it."

"Santa Anna has not stopped it. It is to both our advantages," Juan explained. "Do not worry, Victoria. I will be careful."

She pressed another tortilla into his hands. "Here, take more. There is food enough. The men slaughtered a steer this morning."

He took the food, but his gaze was focused on the door. "Looks like Dumont could use a good meal," he said. "He's just coming off watch."

Victoria glanced up as Jake spotted them and strode toward the table. Cold air swirled off his clothes, and his nose and cheeks were red above his day's growth of dark whiskers.

"*Señorita,* Captain." He removed his hat and hung it on a wall peg. Turning, his gaze on Victoria, he waited.

The angry words from their last conversation hung in the room between them.

"Do you mind?" he said. His voice held little hope for her acceptance, yet he challenged her with his look.

After he'd stood watch half the night, she'd be a witch to deny him a warm meal. Did he think she was that hard-hearted? When she shook her head and reached for another cup, he propped his rifle against the wall and sat down on the bench. Rubbing his hands together, he blew on them and shivered.

"You're half-frozen, Anglo," Juan said, oblivious to the tension between them.

"Temperature dropped. Blue Norther rolled in early this morning."

When Victoria poured the hot coffee into his cup, he wrapped his hands around it and his eyes closed for a moment as if savoring the warmth. Lines of fatigue marked his forehead, and shadows played under his eyes. She served up an extra egg for him along with his beefsteak and wondered if the others would notice. He deserved it. He'd worked hard through the night to keep them safe while many in the fort had slept.

Outside, a man yelled. Diego strode to the door and looked out, then turned back, new urgency in his voice. "They're coming! The Mexicans are coming! A whole mess of them!"

Jake finished the food in his mouth as he shoved his plate back and jumped up. He grabbed his hat, jerked up his gun and raced outside with Juan. Together, they ran across the yard and up the dirt hill to the big cannon. From this point they could see the Mexican army splashing across the shallow river. Splotches of color from the red coats worn by the men showed through the cover of the cottonwood trees as they swarmed toward the huts and adobe *jacales* near the east side of the fort.

His rifle to his shoulder, Jake stared down its sight, trying to get a clear shot. "I hope their toes freeze in that river water," he said, trying to get a bead on them. Others were having the same trouble apparently, since no shots were fired.

"Don't waste your ammunition!" Travis shouted as he joined them to take stock of the situation.

"Those huts should have been cleared out before this," Juan said. "Now they'll use them as cover."

"Too late to worry about that now," Jake answered. He started to lower his rifle but then saw a band of Mexican soldiers break loose from the trees and race into the open toward the fort. "Get ready!" He whipped up his rifle and took aim.

Suddenly the cannon at his side boomed and a shell exploded at the feet of the advancing Mexicans. Rifle fire broke out, splattering bullets across the short expanse of prairie grass and into the forward line of the enemy. Several men went down.

Gunfire erupted from La Villita. The soldiers, hiding behind the huts, tried to draw the defenders' shots off their fallen comrades in the field. Jake heard their excited shouts, though he couldn't understand them, as they reloaded and took aim on the men in the Alamo.

Artillery from the fort boomed. A thick cloud of acrid smoke filled the air between the two forces. The cannon sent shards of metal into the nearest line of advancing Mexicans. Finally, the foot soldiers broke rank and turned back, grabbing their injured brothers and dragged them into the shelter of the village. Once there, Santa Anna's soldiers began firing again, this time taking better aim.

Jake lowered his rifle. It was a waste of bullets to

continue. The soldiers were too well covered. He glanced around the wall, checking each post position. No casualties, thank God. Keeping his head low, he peered over the edge and checked the Texian soldiers in the trench below. They were shaken, but not one man down.

A lead ball slammed into the wall just below him, spraying dust into his face.

"They have the advantage," Juan said, starting down the rampart with his rifle. "And they know it."

Jake matched his steps. "With reinforcements, they could set up more artillery. It won't take them long."

"We have to do something," Diego said.

Jake glanced across the yard searching for Victoria. She was no longer there. Good. Hopefully she had stayed safe inside the kitchen or gone to the church.

A group of men strode from the baptistry where the ammunition was stored. They carried unlit torches and rifles, determination filling their faces as they gathered at the main gate. Crockett walked with them.

"A suicide mission," Jake said under his breath, striding to meet them.

Juan grabbed a torch, but Jake wrenched it from his hand. "Not you, Captain. Your men need you here."

Juan frowned, and then nodded in understanding.

Jake strode over to the fire and lit his torch, then returned to the men and held it high for the others to start theirs. Beside him, Diego struck his torch and his dark gaze met Jake's. Jake saw the fervor inside, the eagerness to prove himself in this act. It was the same look his brother had had just before leaving for Texas.

They both thought they were invincible.

Jake sucked in his breath. Had he ever been that innocent? So full of righteous zeal that he believed nothing could hurt him? Once, maybe, before he'd struck out on his own and found out what the real world had to offer. With a growing certainty he knew that whatever happened outside the walls, he'd watch Diego's back.

Together with Crockett and the others, Jake rushed through the open gate. Crouching low, he raced across the grassland toward the village, his torch streaming smoke and fire. He made it halfway to the huts before the Mexican soldiers realized what was going on and took aim with their Brown Bess muskets. He heard men shouting *juego!* and tightened his grip on the torch as he raced on, keeping close to Diego.

The sound of rifle fire opened up behind him as the soldiers at the Alamo volleyed lead over his head to provide cover. A Mexican dropped not twenty feet in front of him. Jake raced on, but Diego, stunned, froze and stared at the sight of the bloodied young boy. A Santanista aimed his musket at Diego. Jake turned back and dove for the young Tejano, pushing him to the ground and covering him with his body. The Mexican ran up, taking better aim at Jake. A burning pain seared his shoulder near his neck. Jake jumped to his feet, ready to use the torch as a weapon when suddenly the soldier dropped his gun and clutched his chest. He fell not two feet from Jake and Diego.

"Come on!" Jake yelled, tugging Diego to his feet by his coat. He pushed him toward the shacks. Two more Santanistas pulled back to the protection of the cottonwoods.

Ahead of Jake, Crockett arrived at the first hut and jabbed his torch into the wall. Despite the heavy frost on the wood, the fire caught hold immediately, shooting up flames. Then nearby a shed began burning as the fire jumped across the short space and the thatched roof burned. Jake and Diego ran to the second hut and threw their torches inside. A Santanista stepped from behind the shanty and, bayonet at the ready, rushed toward Jake.

Diego fired, and the man went down, a stunned look on his weathered face.

The other Texians raced to the next huts with torches and soon the entire line of adobe and wooden shacks was in flames. Rolling, black smoke obliterated the view of the houses and the enemy soldiers beyond it.

Seeing several of the defenders lower their rifles, Jake called to Diego. "Hold back! They're retreating!"

"We can still get them!" Diego yelled, caught up in the fervor of the chase.

Jake clamped a hand on the boy's shoulder just as

he started to spring away. "And walk right into a trap? No. We've done what needed to be done."

Crockett ran from behind a burning pile of wood and motioned for the men to retreat to the fort.

Convinced at last, Diego lowered his gun. "At least they won't be able to use this place for cover now."

A lead pellet whizzed over his head.

Jake crouched low and dragged Diego with him. "Let's get back," he said.

The men at the Alamo continued to fire over their heads as they raced back to the fort. The main gate opened, and once inside, Jake breathed deeply to catch his breath.

Juan appeared at his side and slapped him on the back. "*Bueno!* You made it!"

"It's not something I'd choose to do again anytime soon."

Juan grinned and then turned to Diego who said something in Spanish. They both laughed.

"What was that?" Jake asked, watching the boy suspiciously.

"I said only that you are getting too old for this. The excitement is too much for you."

"Ten years does not make me an old man. It just makes you a whelp."

Diego grinned again, his white teeth flashing against his darker skin. "Even the great Crockett looks a bit winded."

Juan shook his head. "Easy, now. He's the best shot this side of the Rio Grande. Don't go criticizing our side."

From the church door Victoria watched the men. Relief coursed through her as her heart slowed to its normal rhythm. They were safe. They were both safe.

She had watched Jake and Diego leave, knowing they had to do this and yet so scared they would be injured or die. Every loud shot of a rifle made her jump. Then, as she ran out into the yard, she'd heard more rifle fire and stopped in her tracks, afraid to go farther, unable to face what she might see.

But now it was all right. The three men strode toward her looking winded, yet fit and confident. Juan and Diego laughed at something Jake said. They seemed surprisingly relaxed and comfortable with him.

Try as she might to keep her eyes on Diego and Juan, she couldn't stop looking at Jake. He was taller than the other two, with broader shoulders. She glanced again at his shoulder—blood seeped through his nut-stained cotton shirt, the red patch growing larger by the second, as big now as his fist.

Their voices sounded far off, as though they were a great distance away. Jake looked at her and the laughter dropped from his face as he covered the space between them in a quick stride.

"Victoria! What's wrong?"

She had never seen his eyes so shockingly blue— nor so full of concern. The sky behind him seemed to spin. She could barely breathe. "I'm all right. It's you."

"Me? Victoria, listen to me. Take a deep breath."

Dutifully she did as he said. The frosty air seemed to freeze her lungs on the inside, but she felt better. Her reaction mystified her. She hadn't expected to go faint at the sight of blood. Growing up on a cattle ranch she'd seen plenty of it. Just not this man's, she realized.

"You're hurt."

He raised his brows, not understanding her.

"Bleeding."

He glanced at his chest, smoothing his hand down his shirt. He couldn't see it, not when it was so close to his neck.

"There." She touched him near his neck. The muscle was firm under her finger, the shirt wet from blood.

He shrugged. "Must be just a scratch. Nothing serious."

She rose up on her toes. If he could run out into the midst of a hundred guns, the least she could do was check his wound. "I'll have a look."

She pushed the shirt away until she could see the laceration. In her opinion it needed stitches to close it. But a man—well, a man would scoff at her. Either way, stitches or not, he would have a scar.

"Just burns a little," Jake said, and placed his hand over hers.

Juan stepped close.

Her pulse quickened.

"I think he'll live, Victoria. You can let go of his shirt."

She looked up at Jake. His eyes were full of suppressed mirth. Discomfited, she released his shirt and pushed him away. "I'll just get the ointment from my satchel. I'll be right back." She turned quickly and entered the church.

She walked to her pallet and sank down by her cloth satchel. Loosening the pull strings, she rummaged until she found the jar. But she didn't get up, she just knelt there, the liniment jar in her lap. What had just happened outside? Why did Jake affect her to the point her heart raced at his touch?

She thought back to when she'd first danced with him. How cocky he'd been. How full of himself. All he'd wanted then was a game, a challenge. He meant to show he could sweep her off her feet, maybe win a kiss, and then be on his way to wherever, to find his brother. She wasn't so naive that she didn't know the ways of men in that regard.

Her cheeks warmed as she realized she'd let him have what he wanted—that kiss in the corral. Truth be told, she'd wanted it, too—and had wondered what his lips would feel like on hers.

Her father always said actions made the man— Juan, too. She sifted through the facts she knew about Jake Dumont. First he had helped her into the fort even though he was suspicious of her. Then instead of leaving, he'd stayed. He'd taken his turns at watch and helped buttress the north wall. And today he'd rushed out into the very middle of the Mexican army. He'd done all this when she had thought he was afraid to fight…and had said he had no soul. Perhaps… Perhaps she'd misjudged him.

She looked down at the jar of salve in her lap and took a steadying breath. Applying it meant getting close to him again—touching him. Even now the thought made her pulse jump. Maybe it was best to let Diego apply it.

Coward, she thought. Yet, she didn't want to see him hurt. Administering aide to his wound—that was all she was going to do. Her father would not object to that. He would expect it of her even with one of his ranch hands. Anything more—well, it just wouldn't happen. There was a battle ahead. If they won, which seemed a long shot even with reinforcements, he'd leave to look for his brother. And if they lost…well, she couldn't face that or even think about it.

Either way she had no choice but to keep her distance.

Resolved now, she tore two strips of cloth from a clean dishcloth in her supplies and rose to her feet. Outside, Jake sat against the stone wall of the church with a gourd of water in his hand. She kneeled beside him, avoiding his gaze while Juan continued speaking.

"I don't think Santa Anna will have the guts to try an attack like that again. Not in broad daylight."

"How many did we lose?" asked Jake.

"None! Just scratches on a few. But I counted at least six Santanistas that went down."

"Their muskets are old," Jake said. "And they shoot from the hip—not exactly accurate. We've got better rifles."

"Still they have us outnumbered," Diego grumbled. "We should have kept after them."

"No," Juan said. "Jake read the signs well. It was smart to come back when you did. If they'd lured you farther to the river, you would have been out of range of our rifles here and at their mercy."

Victoria said a quick prayer of thanks that Jake had been with Diego. When she opened her eyes, she found him studying her with an unreadable expression on his face and again was caught in his blue gaze. Behind her Juan and Diego continued talking, oblivious to the current that coursed between her and Jake. Her gaze dropped to his mouth, remembering the soft touch of his lips against hers and then the insistent firmness of his kiss. She swallowed.

Finally she raised her cloth toward Jake's wound. Taking the hint, he pulled his shirt away from his neck.

She wet the first cloth and dabbed at the wound to remove the blood and then applied pressure to stop further bleeding. Then, taking a small dab of ointment with her finger, she smoothed it over the area. A wayward tremor of her hand caused her to brush against his beard and reminded her of the same scratchy sensation against her cheek when he had kissed her. She swallowed and applied the second strip to the ragged abrasion, feeling his gaze searching her face the entire time.

"The ointment will hold the cloth in place for now. You can put your shirt back on."

"Thank you, Señorita Torrez."

She glanced up at his face, grateful that he'd been

so formal with Juan and Diego watching. His gaze held hers a moment, and it seemed that there was more he wanted to say, but then he shrugged back into his coat and the moment was gone. She gathered her supplies and as she moved to stand, he offered his hand for balance. She hesitated, but then took hold, finding his hand firm and warm. Her own hand tingled from his touch.

He indicated the statues at each side of the church doors. "So who are these two? Guardian angels?"

"You do not know?"

She stilled as he reached for the necklace she wore and studied it, feeling the weight of it in his hand. "You forget. I'm not Catholic."

Would he mock her beliefs? Perhaps he would have before now. She didn't think he would today, not after he and Diego made it back to the fort in one piece in the midst of so many enemies. "This," she indicated one statue, "is St. Dominic. Juan says the people here believe he is the patron saint of lost causes."

Jake grunted. "Guess we can use him on our side."

She felt the corners of her mouth tilt up.

"And the other?" he asked.

"St. Francis."

"What is he all about?"

"He has the gift of prophecy and the ability to inspire passionate devotion."

He no longer stared at the statues, but instead, gazed at her. A shiver stole through her. What was going through his head that he looked at her so?

Finally he bowed slightly. "Thank you again, *Señorita.*"

He stayed there, studying the statues, while she walked back inside the church.

Chapter Eight

That evening gunfire erupted behind the Alamo and Jake grabbed his rifle and ran toward it with the others. It was the first skirmish since earlier that afternoon. Santa Anna had decided to wait until dark— probably having come to the same conclusion that Juan had about the Texians' aim.

The smattering of gunfire and shouting ended within a few minutes—but was just long enough to put everyone on edge again. A few more days of this and everyone would be jumping at the sound of a whimper.

Jake sat on his sleeping pallet in the barracks and wiped down his rifle. He wondered what Victoria was doing now. He'd been scared when she went pale beyond belief. If that's how blood affected her, she was in the wrong place. Things were bound to get a lot bloodier before any of them were clear. Still, it had been a lesson in self-control to have her so near, ministering to him and yet not being able to pull her to him and take what he wanted. Her light touch had made him feel weak and yet strong at the same time. He'd wondered, as she smoothed on the ointment, if she would allow more. Not in front of her cousin and Diego, of course, but it had taken all his willpower not to reach up and brush the strand of hair from her cheek and rub his thumb over her soft, full lips.

The air had been alive with energy between them—thrumming, vibrating, energy. She'd felt it, too, and it scared her. He hadn't made it easy for her. And he wouldn't. She was better off without him around. He *was* a bad risk—one that would either be dead in a few days or gone to find Brandon.

He'd made that clear enough.

Angry shouts sounded from the yard. *Now what?* Jake thought as he rose from his cot, rifle in hand, and headed outside. It was dark with the exception of the few campfires burning. A group of men surrounded Travis at the doorway to his office. Juan stood next to him. He didn't look pleased. Something was happening.

"Don't send him, Colonel," a man shouted. "He could be one of them."

"Last time I checked, I was the man in charge here," Travis answered. "The council has met and their decision is final. Juan will get through better than any of the rest of us. He looks the part and he knows the language."

Grumbling broke out again.

"He's runnin' away. Just like the others yesterday when the shootin' started," another man said angrily.

Jake didn't like the set look on Juan's face. He was trying to stay calm.

"Those men were given leave to check their homes and families," Travis said.

"How do you know he's not a spy?" someone else challenged with a dark look. "He didn't head out with Crockett to burn the shacks."

The thought spiraled through Jake that a few days ago he'd have thought the same as the rest of the men. He'd have been suspicious, too. But now he had no doubt of Juan's sincerity. He stepped forward. "Captain Seguín was willing enough. I grabbed his torch and pushed him back. Told him his men needed a leader. I was more expendable."

Juan met his gaze.

"Well, someone is runnin' information," the same man retorted, unwilling to drop the subject.

Travis held up his hand. "Enough. The decision has been made. Seguín goes. He knows this country better than any of the rest of us. If we are lucky, he'll get through the Mexican line and take my request to Fannin in Goliad. Now, this discussion is over."

The rest of the men grumbled, but no one further defied Travis. Slowly the group dispersed. Diego and Jake approached Juan.

"How long will it take you to get to Goliad?" Jake asked.

"Two days' ride. General Sesma has set patrols out east of here, but he has fewer men than the other officers. I should be able to slip through their line. I'll gather men in Goliad and then head to Gonzales to bring more."

"If Santa Anna waits that long," Diego said.

"I think he has reason for waiting. He may hate me—in fact I'm sure he does. He expected me, as a Tejano of property, to side with him. And Crockett is big—even the Mexicans have heard tales of him. But in the end, I believe the general is looking for bigger game than me or Travis or even Crockett. He wants Houston."

"That would crush the rebellion completely," Jake said.

Juan nodded and for a moment stared at the soldiers taking watch. "I hate to leave my men. I belong here with them."

"They know what to do. And you'll return soon." Jake hoped he spoke the truth.

Juan turned back to Diego. "I must tell our cousin."

"I'm here," Victoria said from a few yards away. "I heard."

Jake wondered how long she'd been standing there.

She moved closer. "I understand why the council chose you, Juan. You are the best choice."

"But you. What am I to do with you now?" Juan took a deep breath and let it out. "Your father would have my head if he knew I was leaving you."

"Your task is more important. He would understand." She glanced over at Jake. "Señor Dumont should go with you. He didn't mean to get caught up in this, anyway. And he is good with a gun."

What was she playing at now? Jake wondered. She wanted him to go? That's not what her eyes said this afternoon. "I might get fifty yards before the Mexican soldiers caught up to me. Juan couldn't talk fast enough to escape a bullet then. I'd ruin any advantage he had."

Victoria dashed a hand across her face. Jake looked closer. Was she tearing up? He didn't want to believe it. He'd thought her passionate—yes, and strong to a point of being inflexible—yet after her display of tenderness earlier that afternoon and now her tears…she seemed somehow more womanly than ever. He didn't know what to trust.

Seguín drew her into his arms. "We must all do our part."

After a moment he set her away from him. With a gruff voice he said, "I am hungry. Fix something for me to eat along the way. I won't want to stop."

She tipped forward to kiss him lightly on the cheek. "Be careful."

When she was out of earshot, Juan turned to Diego. "You will watch over her while I'm gone."

Diego nodded and his chest seemed to swell with the added responsibility as he accepted his new role. "I understand my place as her cousin. I do it without needing your order."

Juan clapped a hand on Diego's shoulder. "Things will turn ugly. I hope to be back with reinforcements before then. Make sure my horse is fed, watered and saddled."

Diego headed for the corral.

Juan watched him go and then shifted his gaze to

Jake. The weight of his scrutiny would have made Jake squirm before today. His design had been self-ishly motivated. But today things had changed. Jake met Juan's stern gaze and braced himself to hear what was on his mind. "Victoria has led a sheltered life in many ways. Do not hurt her Jake Dumont, or I will find you."

There was no mistaking Juan's meaning. Jake was to keep his hands off.

"Would you believe me if I said that I only want to protect her?"

Juan's lips twitched. "I think you may want much more than that, *amigo,* but do not act on it. I must trust you with this, and loyalty does not seem to be your strength." He studied him for a moment. "Although I think there is something there. After all, you did come many miles after your brother."

Jake squirmed under the captain's searching look. He did feel that pull in Victoria's direction. Hell—she was beautiful. Any male over the age of one year would want to get close to her. "Don't make me out to be any more than a drifter, Seguín. But I'll do what I can to look out for her."

"Will you give your hand on this oath?"

He looked at Juan's extended hand. To take it would shut out any chance of slipping away on his own. How had Victoria become mixed up in all this, anyway? Why wasn't she safely home at her ranch? Did she know the consequences of what might happen here when she'd come to visit Juan's family? The woman wasn't naive like Brandon. Impulsive maybe—but he'd bet anything her eyes had been wide open when she headed toward trouble rather than away from it. So why did it matter to him that she survived?

But it did, he realized, meeting Juan's gaze. *God help me keep my word.*

He gripped Juan's hand. "In this, Juan Seguín, you can trust me."

Victoria worked that morning in the kitchen melting lead in the fire to make more musket balls for the soldiers' guns. She'd heard Juan say they had stockpiled plenty of rifles and guns in the baptistery, and that there was an adequate amount of gun powder although the quality of the powder was poor. They should be able to hold off the Santanistas for quite some time.

Before leaving, Juan had informed her that Jake would watch out for her along with Diego. It seemed the coyote was watching the chickens, as her father would have said. She still didn't understand why he hadn't left when he had the chance, and she meant to find out, just as soon as she was no longer needed in the kitchen.

By noon her back ached from hunching over the hot fire. It was a welcome relief when she and another woman began the preparation of food for the day. She rose from her stool and picked up two buckets. More water was needed for cooking.

It should have annoyed her—the absolute lack of privacy here. The women had discussed how closed in it made them feel. Now, on the fourth day of their confinement, tempers flared more often. She supposed it had a lot to do with the fact that she didn't have children to chase after and constantly keep out of the way of the soldiers. Rather than annoying her, the close confines made her feel cared for and protected.

She had that same feeling now as she strode across the dirt plaza toward the finished well. A glance around and she spotted Jake talking to Diego by the open fire pit. The scruffy beginnings of a beard that he'd had yesterday had been shaved off. Her pulse quickened at the sight of him.

Why had he stayed? The question burned in her, yet she was afraid to ask him again. Afraid he might answer that he'd stayed because of her—and was now sorry he'd gotten caught in the crossfire for a cause he cared nothing about. Afraid that he might say otherwise. That would disturb her, too, because she couldn't truly believe that he'd suddenly changed his spots and cared about Texas's freedom.

"Victoria!"

She heard Jake's voice, the sound of it overcome by a sudden loud, drawn-out whistling. It grew louder and louder until she thought her head might explode from the scream. She dropped the buckets and covered her ears.

Jake started running toward her and waving his arms. Men in the yard crouched behind posts or dove into the doorways of the buildings. Still Jake raced toward her.

He didn't let up but plowed into her, knocking her down and rolling midair so that she landed on him instead of against the hard ground. Her breath expelled in a rush. Quickly he maneuvered on top of her and covered her with his hard body. Startled, she gripped his shirt and pushed at him—struggling to take a breath. He didn't budge.

The drawn-out whistling grew deafening. This had to be the end. She must be right in the path of whatever had been fired. And Jake had come to her! The thought had her gripping his shirt harder and this time pulling him close while she tucked her face into his chest. She gasped in a huge brace of air as her lungs found their rhythm again.

A shell soared over the fort's wall and exploded just yards from them. Sharp bits of rock, shell, glass and dirt pounded them, stinging her neck and ankles. Every muscle contracted. Shutting her eyes against the raining debris, she felt Jake tuck her against him tighter and grab his hat to shield her even more.

A strange humming filled her head. Slowly she released her grip on him and looked up, dazed. "Say something."

She couldn't hear her own words.

He rose up on his elbows, searching her face. "Are you all right?" he mouthed.

The last of his words broke through as her hearing returned.

Checking to make sure everything else felt normal, she wiggled her toes, her legs, her hips…

A devilish smile creased his face. "Everything seems to be working."

She was still struggling with the fact that he'd risked his life to protect her. The man was crazy! And perhaps impossible.

Concern replaced the smile on his face. "You shouldn't be out here."

"I…I needed water to prepare the food."

A smattering of rifle shots split the air. She grabbed him again and tucked into his chest.

She felt rather than heard a chuckle rumble through him. "It's all right, Victoria. You are safe— at least from their bullets. They don't have enough force to penetrate the walls."

"Then why do they bother shooting?"

"Just trying to keep us on edge."

"It's working," she said, her voice trembling slightly.

"Here," he said, moving off her. "As much as I prefer this position with you, I better help you up before people start talking. I promised Juan I'd see to your reputation."

Her cheeks warmed at his words. She took Jake's proffered hand and let him draw her to her feet. "I heard. *Gracias.*"

"No thanks are needed. Just doing my job." He touched under her chin, turning her face toward him. "Your eyes are as big as the Comanche moon in August."

She glanced at him sharply. How would a man from the east know such a thing? "And you have seen this type of moon?"

"Every time I look at you." His gaze dropped to her mouth. He frowned then. "You were cut. Your chin."

Now that he mentioned it she did feel some stinging there.

"Perhaps you'll have a small scar to remember me by."

Watching the winter sunlight play across his face as he spoke in that deep voice, she couldn't think that remembering him would ever be a problem; however, forgetting him could become one much too easily. She raised her hand to feel the cut, but he grabbed her fingers and held them away.

"I could clean it for you. You did as much for me."

Her heart started up a rhythm completely different than when she had been frightened for her life. His nearness did such funny things to her insides. Those jumping beans again, she thought, as she spread her hand over her stomach. She tried to tell herself that to him, she was only a passing diversion, but it no longer rang true—not since his oath to Juan for her protection. If only he were a man of means or at least of her faith. And if only her parents would accept him into their home. It just could never be.

She turned her face from him, knowing he sensed her answer as he shuttered his eyes with his hat.

"You shouldn't be out in the open," he said again, more gruffly this time.

Diego joined them then, looking her over for signs of injury. "I'm all right," she told him.

"Bueno," he said, his relief obvious.

"I'll get the water," Jake said. He picked up the buckets and headed for the well. When he returned there was a grim look on his face.

Victoria looked from his face to the empty buckets. "What is it?"

He shook his head. "Our water supply has been cut."

The baby in Victoria's arms started to cry. Victoria let out an exasperated sigh. Half the night the Mexicans had shelled the fort, keeping everyone on edge. She'd spent much of it walking this infant, only to have him doze off just as another bombshell exploded. She was ready to cry right along with him. Her arms ached, her legs ached, her back ached.

Another explosion shook the church, and the baby's mother awoke. She reached for her baby. *"Gracias, Señorita Torrez."*

Victoria smiled, letting the baby go to his mother. Finally she could try to sleep herself.

Gratefully, she returned to her pallet and sank down on the thin blanket. Yet there she tossed and turned, unable to get comfortable or warm. Short bursts of gunfire studded the night, first from the east near the stables and then on the west side of the fort. Each time gunfire sounded a baby cried or a child whimpered and Victoria's heart constricted. How could their mothers stand it? The uncertainty, the constant worrying. This was no place for a baby. This was no place for any of them.

She bit back a sob and realized the stress was taking a toll on her, as well. No longer was she able to ignore the constant worry that someone would get shot or hurt by the bomb casings. It could be Diego next. Or Jake.

She rolled up her shawl to use for a pillow, punched it in a few places and lay back down, pulling her cloak up to her nose. It was so cold! She shivered and wished for her room back at the hacienda where Teresa had always heated the sheets with a warming pan before bedtime.

Jake would be warm. The thought slipped through before she could bar it out. He radiated heat. Heat she'd felt in his hands when he'd held her and kissed her. She shivered again.

Squeezing her eyes shut tight, she groaned. *I can't do this. Sleep is impossible!*

Finally she gave up trying and gathering her shawl about her shoulders, rose to her feet. She stepped silently among the other women and children as she made her way to the door. Slipping through, she closed the massive oak-paneled door behind her and tiptoed outside.

The night air was clear and cold. Her breath formed crystals as it left her lips. She stood for a moment, taking in the quiet, wishing it would last, but knowing another firing of a cannon or smattering of musket shot could happen at any time. Men kept watch every twenty feet along the perimeter of the fort, rifles in hand as they lay on the rooftops of the buildings and peered out into the dark.

"Couldn't sleep?"

The familiar deep voice had haunted her dreams, but she was awake now or she wouldn't be so cold. The voice was real. He was real. She turned to him now.

Jake sat on the log and rested with his back against the church's wall, his long buckskin-clad legs stretched out before him. He wore his leather coat, buttoned up tight, his hat pulled low on his head. In the flickering firelight, she could see his features below its brim—the stubble on his square chin, the straight blade of his nose, his glittering eyes. He crossed his arms over his chest, watching her.

She nodded in answer, not trusting her voice. She had hoped that he would be here—needed him to be here.

"Miss me, then?" A taunting grin crossed his lips.

She swallowed hard. "I...I just couldn't sleep. Not with all the gunfire. What are they waiting for? Why haven't they attacked? They are toying with us like a cat plays with a mouse."

"Santa Anna is waiting for more soldiers. His General Cos still hasn't arrived with his contingent."

"But they outnumber us ten to one! And now there is no water! I don't understand."

Just then another report from a single musket pierced the air. She jerked, startled. "Why can't they let us be for the night?" she cried, hating the whine in her voice and the fear that she felt growing. She closed her eyes and willed herself to be strong. She was just overly tired. Her nerves were jumpy, that's all. And she couldn't stop shivering.

When she opened her eyes, the grin was gone

from Jake's face. He studied her with those intense blue eyes. "Come here."

He patted the log beside him. "Sit."

He leaned forward and threw another small log on the fire. As she sat, the wood crackled and hissed. Red sparks flew up, filling the air with the familiar scent of mesquite wood.

"A few men made a run for water tonight. They slipped through the east wall to the lake."

"Did they make it?"

"There'll be enough for another couple days if we conserve it."

She nodded.

"I'm surprised you've done as well as you have," he said quietly, his low voice rumbling through her. "This place is getting to everybody."

She still didn't trust her voice.

"Closer."

A sigh rolled off her lips and clouded the cold air between them as she looked into his eyes. His gaze held no subterfuge, no hint of triumphant male—it asked only that she come closer. It was what she wanted, but...

He raised his nearest arm, giving her a place to snuggle into.

Pushing away the doubts that lingered, she moved into the circle of his arm.

"Good girl," he murmured, and pulled her against his side.

Still, she couldn't relax. Any moment another shot would ring out and she knew she'd jump.

"Tell me about your place in Laredo," Jake was saying. "You mentioned it at the dance."

The dance—that seemed so long ago now. And her home—oh, how she missed it. She sighed, wishing she were there now.

"We raise horses and cattle there along the bluffs of the Rio Grande. The prairie is thick with grass. Small oak trees."

"Good hunting, then."

"Yes. Buffalo, deer, rabbit—"

"Of course," Jake murmured. "There's always rabbit."

She felt a smile tilting the corners of her mouth. "Wildcats."

Jake grunted. "I've had my fill of those. So has Fury."

Just as she'd imagined, warmth radiated through him, heating up everything he touched. With her head against his chest, the beat of his heart penetrated her ear. She closed her eyes and, with a deep sigh, her body finally relaxed against his strong frame. Her breathing slowed as she slipped deeper toward sleep.

"I shouldn't be here," she murmured against the rise and fall of his chest.

He pushed a wayward strand of hair from her forehead and took a deep breath. Glancing up at the starlit sky, he wondered what the hell he was doing as he brought his lips close to her ear. He couldn't seem to help himself. She needed comfort and he wanted to give it.

"Shh," he whispered. "You shouldn't be anywhere else."

Seeing her standing at the door to the church had surprised him. Of course she'd been on his mind. Of late, she was always on his mind. To have her materialize before him, and then let her defenses down enough to let him hold her, she must really be feeling the strain of their situation. Not for a minute did he think she cared particularly for him. She just needed a friend—someone to hold her up when she felt at her lowest.

Well, he would be that friend and more if she wanted. He watched her breath as she exhaled into the frosty air. Her lips were soft, parted a little, her cheek pale. Pushing the persistent strand of rich dark hair away from her cheek again, he enjoyed the chance to look at her. She snuggled closer to him, cocooned between his arm and chest, small and light as thistledown.

He'd protect her, not because Juan had asked him to, but because as much as she hated to admit it, she needed protection. And she deserved it. With all of her high ideals and goals for Texas and the people here, she was a better person than he was. Better by far. The least he could do was look out for her for as long as he could.

He grimaced. That wouldn't be long. Santa Anna wouldn't hold off much longer—a few days, if that much. He was toying with the Texians…just like she had said. Cutting the water supply had been a low blow.

If only he'd met Victoria at another time.

The thought rankled him. She would have hated him. Family and loyalty meant everything to her and here he'd turned his back on both for the past ten years. Jake didn't fool himself into thinking that he'd gotten any of the inheritance. His father could barely stand to have him around. Keeping him fed and dry and clothed had been all the man could tolerate. He thought of the long line of ancestors Victoria spoke of with such pride—all the way back to Spain. He could name only two generations in his family—him and his mother.

No. If they'd met before, he and Victoria would never have exchanged more than a perfunctory greeting and then both gone on their ways. She would have married some high official in the Mexican court or a prominent businessman in Mexico City and visited her family ranch once or twice a year. For some reason, Jake couldn't see her in that life. It was too confining for someone like her. She belonged on that land she loved—riding her horses.

The uprising had changed everything. It brought out the best and the worst in men—and it made it possible for him to meet Victoria. He'd been angry at Brandon for a lot of things—especially for taking off to fight and making Jake chase him halfway across the country. But for this one thing—meeting Victoria—he'd be forever grateful. Even though hope for reinforcements to arrive in time was quickly fading, he was still glad he could be here, beside her, helping her through this.

She shifted against him, and her shawl dipped at her neckline, displaying smooth, creamy skin. Her pulse jumped just below the surface at her throat. In the firelight, shadows danced across her face. The urge to kiss her there, just above the collarbone, gripped him—made his lips tingle with the anticipation. She was beautiful. He'd known that the moment he set eyes on her with that mongrel chasing her heels. The features of her face were perfect—her nose straight and narrow, her eyes large and luminous, and her lips heaven on earth, so soft and inviting and made to be kissed.

Something twisted in his gut, low and primal, bringing to mind that he'd like to do a lot more than kiss her. Something he wouldn't act on. Not now. Not in this situation. Not ever. She deserved better than him.

He tugged her shawl back in place and then slipped his free hand under her knees, rising and pulling her up with him. Her eyes blinked open. "What?"

"Time for you to get some real sleep. On your own bed."

She sighed and her lashes fluttered down as she drifted back to her dreams.

The absolute childlike trust she gave him humbled him. Never had anyone given him such a gift. He vowed in that moment to earn it, to be worthy of it. Somehow.

He strode into the church toward the women's area. It took a moment to locate her pallet in the middle of the room among all the others sleeping this way and that. After gently laying her down, he started to pull away, but her arms skated around his neck and tugged him close.

"Victoria…" A warning crept into his voice.

"Thank you, Jake," she said softly in a sleep-filled voice.

He understood. She hadn't wanted to need him, hadn't wanted to seem weak in front of him or the others. Yet she'd come to him. And he'd given her what she needed.

"Anytime," he murmured, surprised to realize he meant it to the bottom of his soul. How had she come to mean so much to him in such a short time? He didn't want to let her go. It was different than wanting her physically. This urge to care for her, to protect her, went deeper. The thought stunned him— and left him unwilling to delve further.

He leaned down to kiss her forehead. "I have to go on duty now. You're better off here for the night."

When he pulled away, her arms released him of their own accord. She was already back asleep. He watched her for a moment, his mind in turmoil.

He wanted her safe. There had to be a way.

He covered her with a nearby blanket and strode back outside to take his post.

A man who had helped with fortifying the north wall followed him from the yard, an ugly smirk on his whiskered face. "I can see why you are interested in the woman. Get under her skirts if you must, but don't make the mistake of thinking she or the men like her are to be trusted."

Jake's blood ran cold. "I'd be careful how I talked if I were you."

"Only statin' the truth. When the battle comes, they won't watch your back."

Jake grabbed him by the collar. "Señorita Torrez is nothing but class."

"They're all Mexicans in the end." The man spat on the ground.

"Mexicans who are willing to fight for what they believe in." He released the man's collar. "I'd say that takes guts."

The man rubbed his reddened neck. "You got it all wrong, but think what you like. You'll figure it out before long." He sauntered away.

Jake stared after him. He understood the man's distrust. Heck, he'd even felt the same way. Hadn't he thought Victoria might be a spy at one time? He didn't anymore, and couldn't say when things had changed, but something inside told him she wouldn't be here if she was one. Her fervor for a free Texas matched any of the men's here—perhaps more so.

He climbed the dirt hill where he'd start his watch and spotted Diego manning the howitzer there. Jake paused. The young man's eyes brimmed with anger as they looked from Jake to the back of the man striding away. He'd heard the entire exchange. Jake drew up beside him. Nothing he could say now would change anything. People believed what they wanted to. "I'll take watch now." His body tense, his jaw tight, Diego turned and walked away.

Chapter Nine

Jake swung his feet to the floor and sat up, dragging a hand through his hair. He stretched his arms back, wondering why his muscles felt stiff. How long had he slept? He glanced out the window to get a bead on the time of day. The light was all wrong. Disoriented, he rubbed his eyes and looked out the window again. Shadows fell to the east. The sun was setting, not rising.

He'd slept all day! No wonder he felt stiff.

Why hadn't someone woken him? He should have been back on watch hours ago. With so few men, each soldier had to take double turns at guard duty.

He pulled on his leather boots and stood. Something else was different—a strange quiet hovered in the air. Either he'd been so tired he'd slept through the usual sounds of sporadic gunfire—or there hadn't been any.

His stomach grumbled, reminding him he hadn't eaten in nearly twenty hours. Hopefully, there was still some food left for him in the kitchen—and perhaps coffee if they hadn't run out yet. He stepped through the doorway and headed for the latrine behind the cattle pen.

After relieving himself, he walked toward the small fire pit near the church. From this distance, he could see others using the warmth of the fire, but Victoria and Diego were nowhere in sight. Strange for this time of evening. What was going on?

A group of men gathered at the door to Travis's office. Jake headed toward them. A few of the voices from within were loud enough to filter outside. They sounded angry.

"You can't just let 'em go!" said Deter, the big German Jake usually shared guard duty with. That in itself was odd. If he was here, who was standing guard now? Jake glanced toward the wall. A third of the soldiers were gone.

He peered over a few heads into Travis's office. The lieutenant colonel paced the room's width, appearing deep in thought. Diego stood at the doorpost, waiting, his young face drawn and worried. Jake caught his eye, raising his own chin in silent acknowledgment. Diego flashed him a look filled with distrust.

What had happened?

Travis stopped in front of the door. "As I see it, anyone who decides to leave is nothing less than a traitor. Santa Anna is intent upon inflicting disruption and discord in our midst." He looked straight at Diego. "You can pass that along."

Diego turned then, and spoke in Spanish to the

small group of Tejanos behind him. The men grumbled and frowned at his words.

"Are they clear on my position?" Travis asked.

Diego nodded. "*Sí,* Lieutenant Colonel." He hesitated.

"Well. What is it?" Travis prompted.

"A few want to know if they go, will they be shot."

Travis's hands clenched at his sides. "By which side?" he asked sarcastically.

Diego remained silent.

Travis's blue eyes took on a glint of steel. "Tell them they can go. I won't stop them. But I cannot say what Santa Anna will do with them once they leave the fort. I can only trust they will not betray our situation here to him."

"*Gracias,* Lieutenant."

"Dismissed."

Diego turned back to the group of Tejanos as murmurs rose in the Texians behind him. The words "traitor" and *"paisano"* could be heard murmured among the Anglo men. Someone shouted out, "Let 'em leave. We don't need them!" and shoved Diego in the back.

Diego stumbled, but quickly regained his balance. He turned, ready to fight, his dark eyes flashing fire as he gripped his rifle.

Things were coming apart. Jake shouldered his way through the small crowd and positioned himself between the two men, hoping to defuse the tension. "What happened today?"

Diego glanced from the man who had taunted

him, to Jake. Some of the tension eased from his jaw. "Where you been, Anglo?"

"Apparently in the wrong place. No one woke me for guard duty. I was sleeping."

Diego studied him a moment, as if to decide whether to believe him. "Santa Anna has declared a three-day stop to bombing. He wants to give those of Mexican descent a chance to leave the fort. Some—" he glanced at the dog-faced man behind Jake "—are not happy with this."

The German had been listening. "Didn't figure you for a Judas, Jake."

"You don't have me figured at all, Deter. Give it a rest." He knocked shoulders with the man as he pushed through the crowd.

He had to find Victoria. This was her chance to leave.

Night had fallen, and with it the temperature had dropped. A few small fires for warmth lent light to the fort's interior as he strode across the yard. He glanced at the men standing guard on the perimeter. Watch would be hell tonight—cold and miserable, but more necessary than ever. Travis wouldn't lower his defenses further. Santa Anna had to know this new situation didn't mean they'd get lax.

He entered the church and headed to the adjacent room where the women stayed, not caring that he surprised a few of them. He found Victoria deep in conversation with an older woman.

He helped her to her feet without preamble. "We need to talk. And I need to see to my horse." He'd ignored the poor beast all day. He let go of her arm just long enough for her to grab her blue cloak and throw it over her shoulders.

"I gave Fury water earlier when I didn't see you."

Jake stopped, surprised. "He didn't scare you?"

"No. I told you that I was raised around horses." Color came into her cheeks. "And I must have had enough of your scent on me to settle him."

The thought of her small body tucked against his had heat racing through him and something else— that protective feeling again. She looked utterly beautiful as the clear moonlight hit the curves of her face. She'd pulled back her hair into one long thick braid. Rich, dark tendrils curled at the nape of her neck—right where he'd like to put his lips. He steeled his thoughts against his own wants. He had to convince her to leave while she could. And wanting to hold her again couldn't have any part of it.

"I checked his wound. I don't think he will need any more salve. It is healing well."

Jake slowed his stride. He wasn't used to having someone look out for him.

The hint of a smile flitted across her face. She knew she'd surprised him. A man was only as good as his horse in this country and he'd neglected Fury today.

"When will you remove the stitches?" she asked.

"Tomorrow. When there is more light."

"He is a beautiful stallion. My father has one, very similar but not quite so big. I hope Father still has the horse. Not the Santanistas."

He paused. "They were at your ranch?"

"That is how I came to be here. They charged through our land in the middle of the night, making everything tremble. I barely escaped, but someone had to come here to warn Juan."

"That took a lot of guts." He wondered if she was alone at the time, then realized it must have been Diego who helped her. A woman traveling alone wasn't safe in this wild country.

She waited at the entry to the corral while he went after Fury. Grabbing a nearby rope, he walked steadily up to the stallion, threw a rope over its head and led the horse to the adobe lean-to where he poured a measure of grain for him. Then turning to Victoria, he spoke his piece.

"I heard about Santa Anna's proposal. Tell me you are considering it."

The openness on her face shuttered down. "I did. For about one minute. It doesn't change anything."

"It changes everything. You would be safe."

"I can't be sure of that. Anything could happen to me once I leave these gates."

"Diego would look out for you."

A frown furrowed her brow. "I see you've thought it all out."

"Some. The part where I follow you—I haven't worked that out yet."

She raised her palms. "Now you are talking nonsense."

"No." He stared at her. "It's not nonsense. But it does sound impossible."

"Right. Because I'm not leaving. I'm staying here

and Diego is staying with me. Juan didn't ride off to get reinforcements just to return to find all of his soldiers gone."

"He would understand."

"No. He's fighting for his land the same way that I am. I may be a woman, but I'll stay and do my part. I can be here to help the soldiers."

Frustration growing, he clenched his hands. How could he make her listen to reason? She was being so stubborn. "Victoria, I want you to be safe." The words vibrated emotion, surprising even him.

Her dark eyes stared into his as silence filled the space between them. Finally she spoke. "So tell me, Señor Dumont. Why have you stayed?"

"Easy. I promised Juan to look out for you. And don't change the subject."

"This is the subject. Even before your talk with Juan you made the choice to stay when you could have left before the Santanistas arrived. Why have you been here instead of searching for this brother of yours? Perhaps I am right when I say that I don't think he really exists."

"Believe me. He does. And like I said before, a more idealistic kid you'd never meet. He'd fit right into your black-and-white world. He is all for this rebellion. Even though his home is a thousand miles away he had to come take his chances here to see what kind of man he was." He ran a hand through his hair and resettled his hat.

"He sounds wonderful," she said. "The complete opposite of you. You are not close, then."

He huffed. "'Bout as far apart as the sky is to the earth, or an eagle to a rattler."

That made her frown.

"You're the rattler?" She studied him a moment. "And still you have come after him?"

"What happens to all brothers? They fight, they argue."

"They don't ride a thousand miles to fight a war. Not over anything small."

"Brandon—" He took a breath. Why couldn't she leave this alone? This wasn't what he wanted to talk about.

"He is your only family?" she prompted.

"Yes. He doesn't know I'm looking for him. If he did, he'd probably head farther south…or west."

"You must have done something, then. What?" She crossed her arms, waiting.

"That's none of your business."

"Then my leaving here is none of yours. It is fine for you to know everything about me but you don't like it when it's the other way around."

He paced the length of the stall before looking up. "That's not true. I still don't know who that man in your kitchen was."

"That's because you are afraid to believe me! I told the truth—he is a friend."

"Looked like more than a friend to me."

She raised her chin. "A former suitor then."

"Former?"

"See? You question my answer anyway. It does no good to be truthful with you."

"Oh, I believe you. It was pretty obvious the two of you were friendly from the way he held you. Bark on a tree doesn't get closer than that." Now *he* was beginning to sound like a jealous suitor. She wanted the truth? All right, then. He stopped pacing. "You want to know what I did to my brother that was so awful? I kissed his fiancée."

She sucked in a breath. "That sounds like something you would do. You cannot have a woman of your own so you take your brother's!"

"That's not the way of it. I can have all the women—" He let that go as he noticed her dark eyes flash. This was not the conversation he'd planned. "She tricked me…or rather tried to trick Brandon and make him jealous. It backfired—and in a big way—in front of an entire assembly of his friends and colleagues."

"You kissed her in front of all those people?" Disgust filled her voice.

"I won a shooting match against him and got the prize."

"The kiss?"

He nodded.

"And just what kind of kiss was it? A touch? A peck? Or more like the one you gave me?"

"Not on my part." He looked at Victoria's lips, remembering her kiss. Remembering how at first he'd hoped to exorcise the memory of Caroline's lips with it, and how everything had changed from that moment on for him.

"Oh, on hers, then." She let out a huff of warm

vapor into the night air. "I can see how that would upset your brother."

He grunted. "*Upset* isn't the word for it. He left a note saying he was going to Texas. That shooting match was the last I saw of him."

Her fingers drummed against her waist. "But why wouldn't he fight you instead? It doesn't make sense that to get back at you, he leaves. There must be more to your story."

He'd said enough. "The 'more' is between him and me."

A delicate brow arched. "He looks like you? Big? Strong?"

Jake straightened. She thought that about him? "He's younger than me. More slight of build." *Same eyes,* he thought. *Mother's eyes.*

"Then he looked up to you and you let him down."

"Something like that," he said, thinking back to when he'd left home the first time many years ago. "I'm good at that—letting people down."

"A warning to me, perhaps?"

Jake stared at her. "You wanted to know."

She pressed her lips together as she studied him. "Then you have made a mockery of your reputation, Jake, because you didn't let me down when you stayed. I was glad of it. But I want to know. I…I have to know. For what reason did you stay?"

Aw, hell.

He whipped off his hat and ran a hand through his hair again. She was chewing on this like a mongrel with a ham hock. "Victoria, I wanted to leave when

I first arrived. At the dance? You had me pegged dead on. A dance, a stolen kiss—that's all I was after."

"You got those things."

"Yes. I did. I said then that I couldn't understand why people would fight over land that isn't theirs."

"It is mine."

"But I mean for Brandon to travel all the way here for a cause that is not his."

"It was more what happened between the two of you that made him leave. Not any higher cause."

"See, that's just it. You think your cause is above a person's life."

That quieted her. "I guess I do. Loyalty to a plot of ground that has been in my family for generations is more important than my life. It is what that plot of ground means to my family. To our identity. Our heritage. To those who will come after me."

"I have no land holding me like that."

"No roots you mean. Then you cannot even understand it. Why do I even try to explain it?"

The sadness in her eyes tugged at him. He didn't want her pity. He was happy with his life—with the one exception of his brother, he was damn happy.

He took hold of her shoulders, forcing her to look at him. "If this is so important for you to know, you should hear all of it." That got her attention. He took a deep breath. "When I first arrived, I didn't care about your fight. I still don't and I won't lie to make it easier for you to pigeonhole me. What I care about are the people here. I...I care about you."

She stared up at him with those big dark eyes, drinking him in, tugging him as she had since the first day he laid eyes on her. Slowly she raised her arms and circled his neck. Her lips grazed his, soft and tentative.

Remembering his promise to Juan, he tried not to respond. He'd been warned. But her warm breath on his face tickled more than his skin.

"Somewhere in there, where you don't want to admit it, my stubborn *caballero*, you're a good man."

Aw, hell. She had it so wrong. He gave in and kissed her then, pulling her against him, his hands to her back, allowing her no room to get away or break the contact. Not that she seemed to want to.

Her body molded to his, soft against hard, cool against heat. Her sweet mouth tilted up to him, asking for more. He gave it to her, knowing the yearning wasn't all on her part. Not by a long shot. He was sliding, boots and all, into quicksand and wasn't even reaching for a branch to save himself.

She was why he'd stayed. It had nothing to do with getting under her skirts as that crusty old-timer had said. There was more here—something deeper. She was different from any other woman he'd known, and he wouldn't let anything happen to her.

This was her chance. She had to leave. He dragged his lips from hers and set her from him. "Victoria…you have to go. Take this chance Santa Anna is offering."

She looked up, her lips swollen from his kiss, her

eyes misty. Yet even as he watched, her mouth drew into a stern line.

"This is not just about you and me, Jake. It's as big as the entire territory of Tejas. Even Juan understood. That is why he followed Travis's orders. This cause, this thing we are fighting for is bigger than family, bigger than any of us, and we are all caught up in it, Texians and Tejanos alike. We fight for our land, yes, but we also fight for an ideal. Santa Anna has no right to control our lives. Not when he does nothing to help us."

He scowled. "I know all the reasons."

"Yes. The reasons we came together are different for each of us, yet they mean we stand steady until the end—whatever that end may be. We cannot go back. *I* cannot go back."

She was being impossible. "You mean you won't," he said.

She raised her chin.

In stony silence, he pulled off Fury's rope and released him back into the corral. He couldn't fault her for wanting to fight for her beliefs. He'd expect it of a man. It just made him that much more proud of her—and that much more frustrated.

"Dammit, Victoria. Don't do this! Get out of here while you can."

Her brow furrowed as she frowned at him. Then she turned and walked away.

He'd go after her if it meant he could change her mind. But he'd said his piece. He'd said all he was going to say.

* * *

Late that night the sounds of shouting and gunfire permeated the sacristy. Victoria hurried outside into the night with three of the other women. Strangers milled around the grounds, interspersed with soldiers she recognized. Everyone was talking at once— Lieutenant Colonel Travis among them.

Could these be the reinforcements? Victoria walked toward them, her footsteps quickening as she searched for Juan. There couldn't be more than thirty or so. Not nearly enough. Perhaps this was just the first group and more were on their way. She spied Jake coming toward her and hurried to meet him. "Have you seen Juan?"

Jake shook his head. "He's not here."

"Did he send these men? Have they seen him?"

"Yes. He is being detained by Houston but these men came on ahead. It sounds like Houston is not sending any more men."

Her blood turned cold. "But we need more help! We have to have it!"

"I'm sorry."

He reached out for her but she stepped back, shaking her head. She didn't want comfort. She wanted answers.

"Houston refused?" she said again, unable to believe it. "How could he do that to us? How could he live with himself?"

Her eyes stung as she looked at the brace of men, some of them no older than Diego. They'd known the odds before coming and they'd come anyway.

"Dios!" She sank to her knees.

"Victoria!" Jake said, crouching beside her.

"What makes men do such a thing?" she whispered. What made men rush to the aide of people they don't know in what could only end in certain death?

Her throat clogged as she turned to find Jake had moved close. She buried her face in his shirt, breathing in his strength. "Why?" she asked. "Why would they do such a thing?"

When he didn't answer straightaway, she glanced up through watery eyes to find him struggling with emotions himself. His jaw flexed as his words came slowly. "I've told you all along I don't know what makes a man do something like this. Probably half are regretting it now, but here they are. They didn't turn back. Maybe it's like you said," he continued, staring across the plaza. "This whole thing is bigger than us, bigger than just a handful of Texians. It makes men do crazy—" he looked at her "—and noble things."

Chapter Ten

When Victoria walked from the hospital the next day, she thought about the change that had come over the men. The additional soldiers along with the respite offered by Santa Anna seemed to have a two-fold effect on everyone within the walls. Men still lined the rooftops but they seemed a little less desperate, a little more hopeful. Yet that attitude did not extend to their feelings toward the Tejanos. Suspicion and doubt were heavy in their words and in their glances. More than ever, the Tejanos at the fort stuck together.

So much so that it had startled her when the Texians were kind. At the hospital one soldier, not much older than she, had grabbed her hand as she started to remove his head bandage and change it. He'd lost an eye from the debris of an exploding shell two days before, and the old dressing was caked with bloody drainage. "You should go," he'd said, echoing Jake's words. "There is nothing for you here but death."

Her hands shook as she continued on with her task and unwound the cotton bandage. This man had given his eye and possibly his life to a free Tejas. She looked down at the heap of dirty bandages in her lap. "I cannot go," she murmured softly. "I believe in the cause. Can I give less of myself than you have?"

"You'll end up giving a whole lot more before they kill you."

The brutal images conjured up from his words scared her. She'd stayed knowing what could happen. What could a woman do against men who were larger and stronger? She blocked the images from her mind before they could overwhelm her and leaned in to wrap new cotton strips about his head. "I cannot go," she murmured.

The soldier waited until she was done. "Thank you, *señorita*." He met her gaze with his one good eye. It was green, she remembered, with flecks of gold.

She nodded, moving to the next man.

It hadn't been easy. For some reason, each man had reminded her that it could be Diego lying there or Juan. Or Jake. Now as she entered the kitchen, the walls seemed to close in on her as frustration built inside her. Was there no hope for any of them?

She dragged in a calming breath. Focus, she told herself. Focus on what needed to be done. What she could do to help at this moment. One task at a time. Don't think beyond that. She could begin by making more cornmeal.

She looked for the *metate* she'd brought on the day she'd hurried into the fort. The other women had been using it. Many had forgotten things in the flight from their homes as Santa Anna entered the town. They all shared what they had.

She found the stone on a corner work table.

"Will you leave it for us?"

Startled, Victoria looked over at the young woman kneading dough. "What do you mean?"

"When you go. Will you leave the mortar?"

"I hadn't thought to go."

The woman went still. "Oh."

Victoria grabbed a nearby sack of corn and scooped out a portion of the kernels onto the stone. Using the roller, she began working the corn into a fine grain.

The sun sank below the walls of the fort as she worked, making the light inside dim. The physical work had kept her warm until now. She stopped to start the fire in the hearth, a task made simple by taking a smoldering stick from another fire across the yard to light the dried grass at the base of her kettle. As she turned back to grinding the corn, Diego strode in.

For a moment he watched as she worked. "Have you changed your mind?" he asked in a voice too low for the others to hear.

"No, but there have been many who assume I will."

"The same has happened to me, too. Jorge and Alessandro are leaving tonight."

"Does Travis know?"

"No. They're just going to slip out. They're afraid they might be knifed or shot if people know. None of the Anglos know."

He sat in silence for a while, watching her work. Finally, he commented. "I remember watching my mother doing that over and over."

"At our hacienda, our cook Teresa would grind the corn." She tilted the *metate* and poured the contents onto the center of a cloth. Then she reached for another handful of kernels.

"Listen, Victoria. Think about leaving."

She stopped grinding. She hadn't expected this from Diego.

"These Anglos… This is more *their* fight now."

"How can you say that? It is our land we are fighting for. Not theirs."

She could tell his heart was heavy in that he didn't meet her eyes when he spoke. "What if Santa Anna is doing this because he thinks we have been misled by the Anglos, that we have ended up here because we believe they will share the land with us once Texas is its own territory."

"It won't be their land to share. It will belong to all of us."

Diego's dark brows furrowed together as he chose his words carefully. "I've heard talk—in the barracks at night."

She pressed her lips together. She'd heard the talk too—among the women. "Santa Anna is asking us to betray the others who must stay," she said, thinking of Jake.

"He is giving us a way out. There are only a handful of Tejano soldiers left. What difference will it make if we stay or go? You've seen the size of the Mexican army. They have twenty or thirty men to each one of us behind the gate."

"The general is only creating division among us," she argued. "How can you be sure we will be safe on the other side of this wall? How do we know he won't take us away from the fort and then shoot us for our part in the rebellion in the first place?"

"I don't know!" Diego said, exasperation in his voice. "I wish Juan was here."

Victoria sighed. Diego was only eighteen—young in so many ways—yet he'd handled himself as a man over the past days in the fort. His warm chocolate-colored eyes had lost their sparkle since she'd arrived in Bejar. Disillusioned with the coarse, undisciplined men that streamed in from the north, he'd shadowed Juan. But now Juan was gone.

"These Anglos will not remember the Tejanos who fought and died here. They will not remember me. I will have fought and died for nothing." His face looked so bleak it hurt to see it.

She wanted to answer, "It won't be for nothing," but held her words inside. In this they each had to hold to their own counsel.

Diego looked down at his hands. Something still bothered him.

She waited.

He raised his chin and she could see in his look the man he would become one day—if given the chance. "About the Anglo—how do you feel about him?"

"I'm not sure," she answered, cautious as to the turn of the conversation. "He is a brave man. The things he's done here have helped us." She shook her head. "But my father would be furious…"

"Yes. Because he is not Spanish."

She went still at his words, wanting to defend Jake. "He's a good man."

Diego gave her a hard look. "But he does not see it in himself. He is risking his life because of you. Do you always demand so much of another and give nothing in return?"

"I'm not demanding anything!" she said immediately.

"*Sí*. You are. He stays because of you."

"But he promised Juan."

"You see only what you want to see." Diego's voice held disdain. "The Anglo doesn't stay because of the oath he made, although that will keep him here."

"Then, why?" she whispered, afraid of the answer she'd hear.

"You figure it out," Diego said.

She set the stone aside and walked to the doorway, searching the rooftop she'd last seen Jake standing on when she walked across the yard. Although the sky held meager light, she could tell he was there talking to the next person to take over guard duty. His rugged profile drew her—a silhouette against the deeper blue of the night.

"He isn't one to share his feelings easily." She stepped outside as Diego came to stand beside her. "He did admit he cared for me."

Diego snorted. "It is more than that."

"If that is true, I've held him here."

"Yes, you have."

The bluntness of Diego's words made her wince. "I do not want him to stay because of me. If he believed in Tejas, that would be different. But he believes in very little." She took a deep breath. "I don't want him to stay on my account. I cannot live with that."

"If you go, he will find a way to leave, also. Believe me." Diego paused and then added, "Juan would like you safely out of here, too. He said as much before leaving."

"He never wanted me to get caught up in this in the first place." She sighed, scanning the rooftop again. The second man now stood guard. Jake would be coming soon. "Jake is so full of pride, I'm not sure what he will do. But if I leave, at least I will not be part of the problem."

"You do care for him, then."

"Very much," she admitted. "I have been afraid to say anything to Juan or you. There are so many differences between us."

"The only person who needs to worry about that is you."

She shook her head at Diego's naïveté, but couldn't keep his words from lifting her spirits. "That was never the problem. He has not trusted me before this. He saw me once with Esteban and thought I spied for the Santanistas."

Diego frowned. "I don't trust your friend, Esteban, but you a spy? The Anglo and you cannot see what is right in front of you."

An owl hooted nearby as she thought over Diego's words. Her mind reeled with the choices before her. "Perhaps you should pack what you can tonight—" she swallowed hard and met his gaze "—for both of us."

They waited together, watching as Jake approached, his easy stride eating up the space between them. Diego tipped his hat and strode quickly away.

Jake stared after him. "What's going on?"

"He knew I wanted to speak with you." She took a deep breath. "We talked. And I…I think after all, that I will take Santa Anna's offer. Diego will go with me."

"Good." Jake relaxed his shoulders, obviously relieved. He propped his rifle against the kitchen's outer wall.

"I feel like I am running out on you."

Jake shook his head. "There is not much a woman can do against so many soldiers. You've done what you could, Victoria. What you need to do now is live. Live to fight another day. Isn't that what your father decided when the army invaded his ranch?"

That made her hesitate. "You know about that?"

"Juan told me. Where will you go?" he asked. "The Santanistas are at Juan's ranch."

"I heard. But he has other property where we can

stay. Otherwise we will head farther west or south—all the way back to Laredo if we must. What will you do?"

A half smile tilted his lips. "It's easier for you than for me. I've got the wrong last name, the wrong color eyes. Torrez blends in a little more beyond these walls than Dumont."

"But you will try to leave?" she urged.

He stared at her. "Does it matter to you now?"

Her chest was tight with yearning for this man. It mattered very much what he did after this. Whatever it was, she had the dark feeling she would not see him again. Diego's words came back to her then—about how much she demanded while giving little in return. Well, this man had her heart. Her heart! What more was there to give than that?

A cry sprang from her throat as she reached for him. She gripped his collar and pulled him toward her, catching the surprise on his face just before his eyes closed and her lips met his. She loved him. It was as simple as that. Angling his head, he quickly took over, deepening the kiss, pulling her closer.

He groaned, causing her heart to pound in her chest. She felt his tongue against the seam of her mouth and opened to it. Lightning pulsed through her body, and her breath quickened. She would hold nothing back to let him know how she felt.

Just as quickly as it had begun, she felt his hands on her wrists, removing her arms from his neck. He pulled back and stared at her, his hard breathing matching her own. "What the hell am I doing?" he said gruffly.

"Kissing me."

"You know what I mean, Victoria. This cannot happen. Not here."

She glanced beyond the circle of light that came from the kitchen's doorway. It was dark. She couldn't see a thing.

He followed her gaze. "That doesn't mean they can't see us," Jake said, reading her thoughts.

Her cheeks warmed. He was right, of course. They did have an audience. The men standing watch on the cannon platforms would have gotten an eyeful if they'd glanced her way. She let out a shaky breath. "You will try to leave? You will be careful?" she urged again.

"I don't count too much on that."

The thought of him fighting and dying because he had no chance to escape frightened her. Her leaving would mean nothing then.

It would mean you could fight another day, his words echoed in her mind.

Tears burned her eyes as she stepped away from him. If he got away, he would go after his brother. It was what he'd come to do in the first place. "I wish you luck in finding your brother, Jake. Make things right with him. You will not be whole until you do."

He nodded, still studying her. "When will you leave?"

"At first light. Diego is preparing things now."

"Then you better get your things together, too. You and I both know what might happen if you stay here. Seems I can't be near you anymore without touching you. Even now I want more than a kiss."

She looked in his eyes, seeing the steely determination to keep his distance. His hands clenched into fists. She took a step toward him. "But I thought… tonight…for just a little while…"

"No, *señorita*," he said with a rough voice.

She had hoped to be with him, have him hold her as he had the night before. She wanted that. Apparently he didn't.

Confused and more than a little embarrassed, she hurried away from him and into the church.

The last day of Santa Anna's generous offer dawned stark and cold. The sky had barely lightened from pitch-black when, bleary-eyed from a night of little sleep, Jake sat up from his cot and stuffed his feet into boots. He knew Diego and Victoria would leave early, before many in the fort were up and about.

He'd wanted Victoria so badly last night it was a craving in his blood. When he'd ordered her to leave, the look on her face cut through him. She might want a chaste night together like they'd shared by the fire, but he wanted anything but that. Her kiss had ignited a fire that couldn't be stopped by just holding each other. He wanted more. He wanted to show her the things that could happen between a man and a woman.

But here? Within the walls of this place? He rubbed his hand over his face. He couldn't do that to her. He cared for her too much to hurt her like that. Her reputation would be in tatters and he'd be the cause.

He jammed his arms into his coat and grabbed his canteen before stepping outside. He didn't want to miss her. He needed to see her before she left—wanted one last image of her, one last kiss.

The kitchen was dark and quiet this early. A bucket filled with water sat on the long table near the fireplace. He poured as much as would fit into his canteen. Then he splashed water onto his face and neck, using his kerchief to wash the dust and sleep from his face. When he looked up, Diego was watching him from the far side of the table.

"You ready?" Jake asked, straightening.

Diego nodded and shouldered his heavy cotton duffle.

"I'm glad you talked sense into her. She wouldn't listen to a word I said."

"She can be stubborn."

Jake thought that was an understatement. "I noticed. I want her to take Fury."

Diego's eyes widened in surprise.

"Better her or you than the Santanistas. I think she can handle him, but she might need help."

"I know horses."

Jake nodded, relieved. "Good."

"What about you? Won't you need a horse?"

When you leave... Jake understood what Diego implied, but he had little hope for it. "I don't see how I can escape the same ending as everyone else here. And reinforcements, whether they arrive in time or not, will not make a difference against an army of thousands."

Diego's gaze shifted away from his. They were both aware how dangerous it would be for an Anglo to leave. How impossible it would be for him to hide himself on this vast prairie.

After feeding and watering his horse, Jake saddled Fury and led him into the gray light of dawn. He paused when he saw Victoria waiting by the corral. Straight and proud, she looked elegant despite the cloth bag filled with her possessions in her hand. She had plaited her long hair and wrapped it into a knot at the nape of her neck. Her tiny gold earrings gleamed at each ear. But it was the dark circles under her eyes that spoke of a sleepless night for her, too.

She glanced from him to Fury, a questioning look on her face.

Jake turned from tying the reins on the post. "I want you to have him."

"But you will need a horse to search for your brother."

"Then maybe I'll steal him back, once I get out of here," he teased.

"I can't take your horse, Jake."

"Think of him as temporary, then—a promise that I'll come looking for you."

Her dark lashes swept down. "It's too dangerous," she whispered, her voice breaking.

At the stark look on her face all thoughts of teasing fled, and he took her hand and pulled her into the shadow of the lean-to. There, in the dim light, he wrapped his arms around her and held her close, savoring the feel of her one last time. He captured her lips in his, pressing her to him with his hand behind her neck. A lump formed in his throat as he moved from her soft, giving mouth to plant kisses on her cheek, her forehead, her jaw and then back to her lips.

She broke away first. "There must be a way, Jake. I want you to go with us." Her voice carried a soft sob.

"You know I can't."

Tears formed and spilled down her cheeks.

He kissed them away, taking in their salty flavor, memorizing the look in her eyes. That look he'd carry with him. "At least I'll know you are safe."

Diego cleared his throat. "We need to go now. Before the whole fort is awake."

Victoria swiped at her tears and nodded. She reached into her satchel, withdrew the jar of ointment and held it out to him. Her face took on a stubborn light. "You may yet need it."

He set it aside and then, hands on her hips, boosted her onto Fury's back. "Be careful," he said, looking from her to Diego. "Both of you."

Diego led the horse to the main gate. Victoria sat tall, her blue cloak gathered about her shoulders like a shield against the angry looks thrown her way by the men on watch.

A wiry man threw a dirt clod at Diego striking him between the shoulder blades. Diego jerked in surprise and tugged on Fury's reins causing the horse to snort and dance sideways.

Jake strode up to the man and shoved him hard.

"Leave off!" he said through gritted teeth. "They have a right to go!"

The man stumbled, grabbing the wall to steady himself, then turned on Jake. "You heard the lieutenant. Traitors—the both of them. I don't mind the woman goin' so much, but he should stay like the rest of us haf ta."

"You were singing a different tune the other day," Jake stated, remembering how the man had sneered at the few assembled Tejanos in the yard. "Is it a wonder they choose to go?"

Jake turned in time to see the last swish of Fury's tail disappearing through the gate. Irritated that he hadn't seen whether Victoria looked back or not, he climbed the ladder to the top of the roof. From this vantage point he watched her and Diego cross over the bridge and start down the river. A Mexican soldier stepped up to them and grabbed the reins of the horse, keeping the animal between himself and the fort. He said something to Diego and then motioned them on their way. Quietly then, without mishap, they headed out of town.

Jake hadn't realized that he held his breath until Victoria passed the last buildings west of town. He let it out slowly then and turned to the man on his left.

"I'll take guard now."

The man relinquished his post with a lift of his chin, shouldered his rifle, and headed toward the ladder.

Chapter Eleven

At eleven o'clock, shots rang out, startling the men on watch. Suddenly three bedraggled riders galloped right past the slack-jawed Mexican sentinels.

"Open the gate!" Jake yelled from his position on the *galeria.* "Riders coming fast!"

Quickly, men rushed to open the gate for them and stood back as the three made it safely into the fort's enclosure.

The first rider leaped from his horse and tossed the reins to a nearby soldier. He grabbed a rolled paper from his saddlebag and held it high above his head. "Good news, men!" he shouted, and strode to Travis's office as men came running from all corners of the fort.

While the men outside strained to hear what the rider had to say, the word quickly got around that he was James Bonham, a courier Travis had sent out days earlier to enlist help.

Jake, anxious to hear the news, motioned to McGregor, who spoke with another of the riders at the gate. The big Scotsman climbed the ladder to him.

"What's the news?"

"More help on the way."

"Do we know how many?"

"Sixty from Gonzales and more expected after that."

From Gonzales? Perhaps Houston had changed his mind or the declaration of independence had been signed. Then Juan would be among those coming back! He'd find few Tejano soldiers to captain, but there were still enough that needed his leadership.

Jake drew back to his post, settling into a position to wait out the rest of his watch. At the edge of town, Santa Anna's guards now stood at attention, alert and wary. They'd have a difficult time explaining to the general how they'd let the riders slip through. Jake wouldn't want to be in their shoes right now.

He wondered where Victoria and Diego were by now. Juan's ranch was a good stretch from Béxar. He looked up to see the sun straight overhead. They wouldn't be at the ranch yet. Maybe by early afternoon, depending on the terrain.

All morning long as he stood watch, he'd steeled his mind against her image. He didn't need the thought of her muddying up his intent to stay. Unlike her, he'd had little choice of whether to go or not.

He wasn't much of a praying man, but he found

himself whispering, *Please, God, let her be safe. Let this all be worth it.*

That night, Jake took his meal with the other men near the barracks. The word was that six hundred more volunteers were on their way. A cheer erupted when Travis announced it. They just had to hold out a little longer and help would arrive.

If Santa Anna's word could be trusted, this was the last night of the moratorium. Already the men were starting to get edgy, wondering when the gunfire and bombing would resume. They all had a deep-seated premonition that this would be the last time.

Restless himself, Jake shouldered his rifle and walked across the yard. He climbed the ramp to the northwest corner of the fort. The sun had set hours ago. A man, one of the three riders who'd entered the fort earlier that day, kept Crockett company next to the cannons. He looked to be about fifty, weather-hardened and tough. His wiry gray hair bushed out to his shoulders from under a battered tricorn hat.

"Put you to work so soon?" Jake asked.

"Can't stand being idle. Feel like something's afoot."

Jake nodded. He felt it, too. Despite the news, he didn't feel much hope. How long could they all hold out against so many? Maybe an hour? Even if help did arrive, they were still outnumbered. He took some solace in knowing they were better trained and better shots than the Santanistas.

The man held out his gnarled hand. "Russell Andrews."

Jake shook. "Dumont. Jake."

Andrews studied his face. "Dumont you say?"

Jake nodded.

"Sounds familiar."

"You've heard it before," Jake said cautiously, almost afraid to learn where and how.

"You got kin helpin' fight?"

"Possibly."

"Young buck. In Gonzales last week. I bought him a beer. Looked like he could use it."

"Did you get his first name?"

"Not to remember. Just went by Dumont. And he had your look about him."

After all this, to hear news of Brandon stunned Jake. "How was he?"

"Fair to middlin'. Got caught in some skirmish just south of town and took a beating. Looked to be healing good enough."

Jake wondered what "good enough" meant to this wizened old man who, by his bulbous nose, appeared to have had one too many run-ins with the bottle.

"Claimed he was a doctor, so I guess he knew what he was talking about. His mood was bothering him more than his health, anyway. Mad as a bee in a bonnet. Wanted to stay with his men, but had to lay up to rest."

That sounded a bit more like the brother he remembered. Brandon had never had a problem with loyalty. He'd possessed enough for both of them and then some. "Did he say where he was headed next?"

Andrews motioned for Jake to keep quiet and pointed to the trees along the river. He raised his rifle.

Jake followed his aim. Tejanos—two of them, along with two women—crossed stealthily through the cottonwoods.

"What are women doin' running with them?" Russell lowered his gun.

Crockett brought the man up to speed with the armistice Santa Anna had declared.

"Well, that explains it, then."

"What?" Jake asked.

"The way the men are acting. Like caged wildcats pacing back and forth."

"Can't say as I blame them," Crockett said. "Don't like being holed up here myself. I'd rather take my chances out in the open."

"Without reinforcements, it won't make much difference," Jake said.

"You're right about that. But like Travis said, they are on their way. The first group is expected tomorrow." Crockett took a deep breath and watched his vapor rise into the cold air. "So what are you gonna do, Jake? You finally got a lead on that brother of yours. You goin' after him?"

"And be labeled a deserter?" Jake shook his head. He'd never get through the Mexican line. But the idea Crockett had planted took hold. The whole purpose of coming had been to find Brandon. And now he had information on him—week-old facts— but better than nothing. He stared out into the night, noting the location of campfires dotting the town and the woods along the river.

Hadn't he always said that this battle didn't concern him? That the outcome of the Texas territory—whether it became an independent country or whether it remained with Mexico—made no difference to him in his life? And now, with Victoria safely away, his promise to Seguín had been kept. Diego would see to her.

"Look there, Dumont—" Crockett pointed to the north wall "—the Mexicans are keeping their distance and holding back over there. Probably to lure runners in that direction. I'd keep away from there—if I was runnin' that is."

"Are you trying to make this easy for me?" Jake asked, his eyes narrowing. "Seems you'd want me to stay."

"Just playing the devil's advocate."

Jake paced the length of the dirt mound, unable to believe where his thoughts were heading. Then looking up he found both men studying him.

"Ain't no one gonna think less of you," Andrews said.

"I might," he mumbled. He climbed down the ladder, putting distance between himself and the two men. He had some thinking to do.

Heading to the barracks, he sat on his pallet and opened up his saddlebag. Inside, he found Brandon's medical bag, a bit worse for wear now that it had traveled halfway across the continent on the back of his horse. Tucked inside was the note Brandon had left his fiancée.

Caroline,
Today you made it obvious you want a different kind of man than me. One more like my brother. I'm going to Texas with Tom. It will give us both time to think things through. The fight should only last a few months, and then I'll be back. Who knows? Maybe I'll be a better shot—for both of us.
Always,
Brandon Dumont

A pang of guilt slashed though his gut as he read it. He'd been the impetus to cause his brother to leave home. He and Caroline both, and he'd never forgive himself if something happened to Brandon.

As an older brother, he'd done a rotten job of looking out for him so far. If Brandon died fighting there'd be no one left to manage the family estate—or carry on the Dumont bloodline. Jake ran a hand through his hair. And then there was Caroline. Hadn't he promised her he'd bring Brandon home?

What to do had never been an issue before. He'd felt compelled to watch out for Victoria. Now he resented the pull he felt to stay with the men at the fort. Hadn't he helped them enough? Building up the north wall? Standing watch? Burning the huts?

A churning began in his stomach that had little to do with being hungry and more to do with guilt. He ignored it. As far as he could see, he had three choices.

He could do what his heart was telling him to

do—escape and catch up to Victoria and Diego. It would be risky considering the number of Santanistas between the Alamo and Seguín's ranch. Just having an Anglo with them would put them all at risk.

He could do what his head was telling him to do—escape and head to Gonzales to find Brandon. Or he could remain here and fight.

No matter which decision he made he would let someone down and probably die anyway.

He stood then, walked to the door and stared at the plaza. Remnants of broken cannon shells littered the yard. On the rooftops, men lay on their bellies taking their turn at watch. Jake rubbed the back of his neck. He was damned no matter what he did.

Refusing to give it another moment's thought he stuffed the instruments back into the bag, followed by Victoria's salve, then his comb, razor and soap. He'd been here long enough. One man would not win or lose the battle that loomed. It was time to see to his promises.

Time to go after Brandon.

Standing, he slung his bedroll and the leather medical bag over his shoulder and strode through the door, avoiding the firelight and keeping to the darkest shadows. The wall on the north would be the easiest to climb over and disappear into the brush, but remembering Crockett's warning, he decided against going there. Instead, he headed to the corral.

The guard was just changing as he neared, the men talking and bantering. The armistice would continue until sometime near dawn which caused the men to be less attentive now. Maybe the Santa-nistas would also be sleeping hard. There was little to shoot at, and the extra men in the fort made it easier for one to disappear. At least, that was his plan.

Jake walked up to stand quietly by the wall. He dropped his pack through a small opening—the one the men had slipped through when they made the run for water. No one noticed the soft thud it made landing on the ground on the other side. Waiting until the guards were caught up in conversation, he quickly slipped through the opening, landing with a jolt on the other side. There was no turning back now. He kept his body low and ran across the grass until he found cover in the tall dried rushes growing along the edge of the lake.

He moved along the edge of the water, staying to the thickest part of the tall reeds. A breeze rustled them, the noise helping to conceal him more. The fastest way to Gonzales would be to travel parallel to the dirt road.

He was nearly there. Just a few more rods.

An owl hooted. Then someone laughed.

Jake froze, his heart in his throat.

A handful of Mexican soldiers gathered on the dirt road.

Inching backward, he drew farther into the high brush and waited, listening to their Spanish—trying to make out any words that sounded familiar, to gain an understanding of their plans.

He pulled more brush over him and waited,

fighting the cramps in his legs as he crouched in the reeds and tried to ignore the cold slimy water that seeped into his leather boots.

After a while the soldiers moved on, dispersing to their own campsites.

Jake allowed himself a moment to breathe—to relax. He would need a horse if he was to get away, preferably one on the outskirts of the Mexican line. To take one before then would only make half a dozen soldiers on horseback come after him. He could be patient. He'd wait until the moon was lower in the sky.

Before any shade of gray had stretched across the sky, Jake made his move, slinking across the stretch of open meadow to the copse of trees by the river. Following the bends of the San Antonio River, he kept to the cover of the elms and willows along the banks until he came across a horse tied up for the night. He eased it away from its sleeping owner and led it a few rods upstream before mounting and kicking it past two sleepy guards. North. It was not the way he wanted to ride. Gonzales was due east and a good sixty miles or more as the crow flies, but over open land according to Diego. Jake couldn't take the chance of getting caught.

As the sky lightened, he turned east and kicked his horse into a lope across the tawny mesquite grass.

The small hunting cabin on the far perimeter of the Seguín ranchero had not been used over the winter. Victoria did what she could to find the stored food and remove the layer of dust that had accumulated on everything. She tacked leather over the windows so that the light from the small fire would not shine out into the night and yet they could still keep warm. During the day there would be no fire— the smoke would be too easy to see and give away their position.

Diego came through the door with a load of wood and set it down. He knelt by the grate and placed kindling to be ignited later. Victoria said a quick prayer for him. His presence had eased her fears over the past two days. She would be forever grateful he had chosen to come with her.

Footsteps sounded on the porch and he jumped up, his gaze landing on the rifle propped near the stone fireplace. It was too far away to be of help.

Two Mexican soldiers burst through and aimed their muskets and bayonets, one on her and one on Diego. They were quickly followed by Esteban.

Victoria gasped, then quickly shut her mouth. She didn't know whether to acknowledge him in front of his soldiers. She chose to keep silent. Diego followed her example.

Esteban looked fierce and commanding as he paced the length of the one-room cabin, his hand on the hilt of his sword. He had lost more weight, but that only made him more severe and forbidding.

"Señorita Torrez. Do not be afraid. And Diego Estrada. I see you, too, came to your senses and chose to take the amnesty offered by our great *presidente* and general. In return for our leniency, however, you must now do something for me."

Despite his words of reassurance, Victoria was frightened. Esteban was not the same man in front of these soldiers as the one who had spirited her away from her hacienda. This man was a stranger.

Diego moved to stand beside her. "What is it you expect, *Capitán?*"

"You will stay here," Esteban continued. "With my blessing of course—and a few guards to keep you safe. When the attack on the Alamo is over I will return for you. Do not try to leave. If you do, you will be shot."

He bowed and strode out through the door.

Chapter Twelve

Jake rode into Gonzales early the next afternoon. The town hugged the banks of the Guadalupe River in the shade of the tall elms, the homes and shops constructed of wood.

He rode his horse to the stables and made sure the animal had oats and water. The gelding wasn't as fast as Fury, but he'd served him well. A man forking straw from a wagon pointed Jake in the direction of the troops' quarters.

As he walked down the main street, Jake was hopeful for the first time in more than two weeks that he'd find Brandon and get him out of Texas and the bloodbath that was sure to come. If he had to knock his brother out and drag him home, he'd do it and not feel guilty. Brandon might hate him for the rest of his life, but at least Jake would be sure his brother was safe in Charleston where he belonged. The inheritance they'd argued over didn't mean anything to him anymore. He had survived for the past ten years without it. He'd make do as he always had—scouting and hunting. And if Brandon no longer welcomed Jake in the family home—Jake would live with that. Just knowing that he was all right would be thanks enough.

He stopped at the first cantina he came to and searched the room for his brother. The odor of cooking eggs and bacon stopped him. He had to eat. He'd gone a day and a half without anything but the water in his canteen. He ordered from a young girl, and sat back to watch every individual that stepped through the door as he ate.

Back on the street he found himself looking at each man he passed, searching for Brandon. He was so intent on his mission that when the door to the mercantile flew open and a blond woman stepped out, pulling her young charges with her, he nearly broadsided her.

"Excuse me, ma'am," he said, stepping to the far side of the boardwalk.

She righted herself quickly and frowned at him before grabbing the hands of her two children and stomping off in the opposite direction.

As he watched her go, he heard a familiar voice.

"Dumont! What are you doing here?" Juan said, stepping away from two men and approaching Jake. "You are here, alone?"

Jake nodded.

Juan said goodbye to the men before returning to Jake.

"Diego? Victoria?"

"They are well." He hoped he spoke the truth. The farther away he'd ridden from Béxar, the more worried he'd become. Diego was a decent shot, but anything could happen with the country overrun with Santanistas.

Juan let out a slow breath. "Come, tell me news of the fort. How goes it with my men?"

"Should I be talking to Houston, too?" Jake asked.

"He's not here. He rode out a few days ago." Juan moved closer. Keeping his voice low, he said, "Tell me what is happening. Why have you come, Jake? Did you desert?"

Jake bristled under his judgment. "I can't desert if I didn't sign up in the first place. Why haven't you gone back?"

"Houston has ordered me to stay here."

"I don't see any ropes on you."

"I follow my orders," Juan said flatly. "Houston refuses to send more help. He believes there is no hope for the men there, but that there is still hope for independence." Frustration marred his voice.

This was difficult for him, Jake realized. Juan felt a duty to be with his men.

Juan backed up a hair's breadth. "All right. What's going on? How did you get away?"

In a few short words Jake explained about the three-day moratorium that Santa Anna had decreed and how he'd escaped.

"You were lucky," Juan said, shaking his head in wonder. "I was stopped twice by soldiers before leaving town. Had to talk my way clear of being shot. Being Spanish, they decided they'd rather believe me than shoot one of their own countrymen."

"We looked for you in the group that arrived."

"So they made it. There won't be more."

"But Bonham arrived two days ago. Said there were six hundred on their way. It's the first hopeful news the men have had in over a week."

Juan furrowed his brow in concentration. "I haven't heard of more than the first group. Six hundred? That is news to me."

For the first time, Jake felt doubt. "Perhaps they are coming from another town?"

"Could be. I did hear something about Goliad. And you say that Victoria and Diego left together?"

"They headed toward your ranch."

"Soldiers are probably still at the main house. Diego knows of other places on the property he can take her. I'm surprised she left at all. What could have made her suddenly decide it was better to go than to stay?" As he said the last, he raised his dark eyes to Jake's.

Jake squirmed under his sudden investigation.

"You would have stayed and fought because of her," Juan continued, studying Jake. "But with her safely away, and no longer in need of your protection, you felt released from your promise to me."

A cold silence filled the space between them. "Put that way, you make me sound like a weasel. Like I don't care about what is happening there at the fort— or to Victoria."

"You've always made the first part quite clear."

"Then you're saying my leaving the Alamo makes me a coward."

"That is a matter you will have to come to terms with in your own time. The situation there is untenable—one from which there is no honorable escape."

Jake studied the group of soldiers walking toward them as he listened. Brandon wasn't among them. "I knew when I made the decision to leave that living with it would be the hardest part."

"*Sí.* None of this has been easy," Juan said. "And Victoria, she cares for you more than I suspected. By leaving under the armistice, she allowed you to leave, too."

Jake ran a hand through his hair, feeling the nerves under his skin jump. He couldn't get her out of his mind. That much was sure. He'd thought putting distance between them would lessen the guilt he felt for leaving her, but it had only made him worry about her more.

"There is something you should know," Juan said. "Before coming here, on the road to Goliad, I came across your brother."

Irritation mushroomed inside Jake. "And you are finally getting around to telling me this now?"

"He was under orders. On his way there with two soldiers."

"Did you mention that I was looking for him?"

"Yes."

Jake waited. When Juan didn't continue, he knew. "It didn't matter, did it? He followed his orders."

"He thought he could help you more at the Alamo by going to get Fannin's men from Goliad. The others that accompanied him didn't think Fannin would budge. When I learned of their mission, I turned and came north to Gonzales to gather men here."

"So he knows I'm looking for him. And he's well enough to ride."

Juan nodded.

Jake sat back, taking in this new piece of information. *So close.* He'd come so close to finding Brandon only to have him slip through his fingers. He understood his brother's rationale—the boy was thinking like a soldier, but that did not make it any easier for Jake to stomach his actions. Every time Brandon put distance between them, Jake felt it like a personal rejection of him.

Who was he kidding? He had no family. All he had was what was here, what was now.

And he loved Victoria.

He stared at Juan, trying to gauge how his next words would be taken. "I'm going back."

Juan's jaw tightened. "You are not good enough for her, Anglo."

"I know that," Jake growled. "The least I can do is make sure she is safe and keep her that way as long as possible. I don't expect any more than that."

"What about your brother?"

Jake chose his words carefully. "He made his choice when he left home. I'm going to let him live with it."

* * *

Jake couldn't believe that he'd arrived in Gonzales only to head back the same day to Béxar. He exchanged horses with another soldier in Gonzales and traveled with Juan and two other Tejanos. As they neared Béxar, the eerie silence started to bother Jake. He had listened for the eighteen pounder at noon. By the length of the shadows it had to be later than that now and still he hadn't heard the boom.

With only an hour of daylight left, they breached the ridge several miles from the town when black smoke suddenly wafted into the afternoon sky in front of them from the Alamo compound. An ugly premonition built inside. They urged their mounts down the hill, only to pull the reins up short when they recognized two men riding toward them as Tejanos from the fort. Juan hailed them in Spanish.

After speaking a few moments, Juan made the sign of the cross over his chest. The two others that had ridden from Gonzales did the same.

Something was terribly wrong. "What did they say?" Jake asked, watching the two men depart.

When Juan didn't answer, Jake coaxed his horse closer. "Juan?"

"It is over," he said quietly.

Jake looked again at the smoke billowing into the sky and blowing to the north. From here he could see the outbuildings of the town and the walls of the fort.

"Santa Anna attacked at dawn yesterday."

Jake felt like he'd been gut-punched. "What about survivors? Did they mention any survivors?"

"The women and younger children." He looked sideways at Jake. "No men."

A heavy weight squashed the breath from Jake. All those men from Gonzales, the big German and McGregor. He closed his eyes, afraid of the answer to his next question. "And the fires?"

Juan's voice was raw. "The bodies."

Jake sucked in a breath. No burials, then—the Catholics, Protestants—all burned in a heap like pagans.

"Santanistas have the run of the town and mission now. From the sound of it, Santa Anna lost many soldiers."

"Good," Jake said, his voice bitter.

Juan sent him a sharp look. "They were my coun—" he said, and then stopped. He swallowed hard, gulping air as though trying not to vomit.

Jake realized, then, the difference between the two of them. He couldn't understand what Juan was going through, not totally. Jake didn't have men he knew on both sides of the battle. Juan had friends, maybe even family he'd known all his life who had been fighting against the Alamo defenders. And as captain of the Tejanos he'd rallied his men to the fort and then not been with them at the end.

Jake kept silent after that, allowing Juan a measure of his grief. He didn't envy him his position in this conflict. If Jake would have trouble living with his decision to leave the fort before the battle— and he knew he would—Juan would have even more.

And what of the man he'd seen talking to Victoria

just before the rush to the fort? Did Juan know him, too? Had he lived or died?

He thought of Victoria and her fierce love of her land and realized that her people, loving and caring for the land from one generation to the next had imbued her with an inner strength that had been growing from before her birth. It had everything to do with her roots. They made her strong, he realized now. And he had to know that she was still strong.

His horse snorted and sidestepped, swishing its tail. "How do I get to your ranch? I need to make sure Victoria and Diego are safe."

His words pulled Juan back from his grief momentarily.

"Santanistas could still be there. It's too dangerous."

"She said she'd head back to her land in Laredo if she couldn't stay on your property. How far is that?"

"Six or more hard days' ride southwest."

"Then I'll head that way until I find them."

Juan shook his head. "I cannot join you in this. I am still captain in the army."

"But your army is dead."

Another sharp look from Juan. "This is but one battle—not the end of the rebellion. I will return to Gonzales. Houston will have orders for me."

Jake couldn't believe what he was hearing! How much could one man endure in this war? Juan had lost so much.

"You've done enough, Juan."

"I should have been there—" He looked once

more at the town. "This isn't over. It may never be over for me."

"Look at the smoke. There is nothing left."

"Do not worry. You don't have to join me. Your heart has never been in this. I've always known that." He gave Jake directions to his hacienda then clasped his hand on Jake's shoulder. "Think on this—if she loses her land because of this rebellion, what will happen to her?"

He watched as Juan once more stared solemnly at Béxar and made the sign of the cross over his chest.

"If you find her, remember your promise to treat her well."

Then Juan spun his horse around and with the other two riders headed back to Gonzales.

Jake surveyed the town of Béxar and the outlying countryside. From this ridge he had a commanding view. The trees along the San Antonio River would give him cover as they had when he escaped the fort, but they could also harbor soldiers. He'd have to go far to the north, to the hill country, and then circle around. He kneed his horse and veered along the ridge.

It would take a long time, more than a day, and that bothered at him. He might miss Victoria altogether. But he had to know. He had to see her. He didn't question what it was that drove him now. It was just there, a need so desperate he could barely breathe thinking she might have come to harm and he hadn't been there to help her.

She'll turn you away, a voice said inside him. *You left her. What does that say about you?*

Guilt stole over him. He squared his shoulders. I'll make her understand. *I won't let her down again. That is my promise.*

Chapter Thirteen

Jake tied his horse in the small stand of pine trees three hundred yards from Juan's house. Actually, *house* didn't come close to describing it. He'd been riding on Juan's land for the past half hour. Now looking over the corrals and outbuilding, it was easy to see why Juan would fight to keep it.

The large stone hacienda was built in a *U* shape around a stone patio. The two-story structure had iron grills over the downstairs windows and a matching wrought-iron gate. Fancy stonework and a massive wooden door graced the front. It dwarfed the home in Charleston where Jake had grown up.

If Victoria's home were anything like it, Jake was amazed she had endured the meager provisions at the fort without complaining. A log for a chair? Straw for her bed? For days she had tolerated it without a negative word.

Two horses stood in the corral, stomping their

hooves. They looked haggard and worn—not the best of horses. Probably belonged to two soldiers, not Juan. Anything of quality would have been confiscated long ago, when the army first arrived.

He waited for an indication that Victoria was inside, hoping it would arrive soon. Twilight left little time and he chafed at having darkness descend before having his answer.

Someone lit a candle near an upstairs window. Jake moved closer, still keeping to the cover of the tree boughs. A feminine giggle floated out on the breeze followed by deep raucous laughter. His heart lurched.

But no—it would not be Victoria.

The front door swung wide with a bang, and a short, stooped man in homespun cotton clothes was forcibly pushed out. He turned and shook his fist at the man who'd shoved him, yelling in Spanish. The soldier in uniform laughed, made a short remark and shut the door. Getting to his feet, the old man picked up his hat, slapped it against his thigh to remove the dust and started to leave. He stopped suddenly to stare at the copse of trees hiding Jake.

Jake pulled back and held his breath, listening all the while for advancing footsteps. When he felt it was safe to look again, he peeked around the tree trunk. The man had tiptoed over to the corral.

Quietly he drew up the rope that looped over the post, and then slowly opened the gate. Was he insane? Get caught with one of those horses, and the soldiers would shoot him down without remorse.

Moving inside the corral, the man shooed the horses through the gate and then ran off toward the east.

Jake moved behind the tree and slowly made his way back to his horse. The bay gelding nickered as he approached. Jake didn't believe Victoria was inside the house. He'd move on. Another—perhaps better idea was forming.

He picked up the trail of the peasant quickly in the dimming light and urged his horse faster. When he spotted the man in a small clearing ahead, the man broke into a run. Jake raced up on the horse and grabbed him by the collar.

"Aye! No!" The man held up his hands, his feet dangling.

Jake dropped him on the dirt and leveled his pistol on him. "Was there a woman in the house?"

Again the man held up his hands. *"No Ingles!"*

"En la casa! Señorita?"

"No, Señor! Solo soldadera!"

Jake couldn't understand the man. His irritation built by the second. He'd distinctly heard a woman's giggle coming from the window.

Frustration threatened, but then he heard a low voice coming from behind a nearby boulder. "He says that only a prostitute is at the hacienda, Anglo."

Peering in that direction, Jake swung his gun around. "Who is there?"

Diego stepped onto the path.

Immediately, Jake lowered his gun. The older man stepped back, uncertainty written on his weathered face as he glanced from Diego to Jake.

Diego lifted his chin. "Ramón."

"Diego."

"You know each other," Jake said.

"My uncle."

Jake relaxed and holstered his gun. "Is everybody related in this territory?"

Diego spoke to Ramón, and the man gave Jake a suspicious look, before glancing at the backdrop of trees behind them.

"He asks if you were the one spying on him at the *hacienda?*"

Jake grunted.

"You are alone?"

"Juan was with me earlier."

Diego looked around sharply and lowered his voice. "Where is he now?"

"Heading to Gonzales."

"Then he is still alive." The young man's shoulder's relaxed slightly. He moved closer to Jake. "You should not be here, amigo. You are not welcome."

He hesitated at Diego's attitude. He told him to leave and then in the next breath called him a friend? What was going on? Jake didn't know what to make of it. "The Alamo has fallen. I saw the fires."

"*Sí*," Diego said, holding his face immobile.

His initial reaction—or lack thereof—surprised Jake. Maybe he needed more time to take in the things that had happened over the past week. It was a strain on anyone, let alone someone as young as Diego. Unless…

"Had you already heard?" he asked.

Diego shook his head. "No, but it was inevitable."

"I want to see Victoria."

"That is not a good idea. She is my responsibility and she needs time to recover from this news."

"Then I should be with her." He wasn't sure what was going on, why Diego was acting so strangely, but he would not let Diego stop him. "I have to see her."

An owl hooted, and Diego's gaze shifted to a point over Jake's shoulder. His mouth tightened imperceptibly. He exhaled into the air and looked back at Jake with a frown. "Follow me, Anglo." He headed into the brush.

Jake grabbed the reins of his horse and followed, ducking under the low limbs of a young oak tree and trying to keep Diego in sight. The land here had more hills, the soil rockier than closer to the river. Boulders sprung up out of nowhere here and there along the Indian trail.

He rubbed a hand over the back of his neck, realizing he was nervous. The thought startled him— after all he'd been through in his life, he was nervous of this woman. What would she think of him after all that had happened? What would he do if she had come to her senses over the past few days? If she realized they'd given each other comfort in a time of stress and that now she should turn him away? The thought troubled him.

They walked half a mile before coming to a small clearing where a one-room log cabin stood. A porch ran the length of it and covers draped the windows, blocking out any light.

"She is inside," Diego said. "I'll take your horse to the shed."

Jake handed off the reins and with it let go of the concerns he had about Diego's strange behavior. He would deal with that later if necessary. For now he couldn't wait to see Victoria. He stepped up, his boots loud as they crossed the wooden planks.

He knocked once on the door, then pushed it open. Victoria stood there, her feet set wide apart, her hair tied back loosely with a dark red ribbon and tossed over one shoulder. Behind her, the small flames in the fireplace danced wildly.

And she held a rifle aimed straight at his heart.

"Jake!"

She didn't recognize the strangled cry as her own. She'd thought him dead—dead with all the others at the fort. Could it really be him and not a ghost she'd conjured up from pure wanting?

"You are alive? I…I thought…I was expecting Juan! But how?"

"Darlin', I'd come a lot closer if you'd point that gun in another direction."

She stared down at the rifle in her hands as if seeing it for the first time, and then looked back at him, dazed. "But I have no bullets."

In one fluid motion he strode inside and grabbed the gun, setting it with his own against the wall. "It is little defense, then," he murmured, undeterred.

Shutting the door with his boot, he dropped the latch into place and then pulled her against him. His arms slid around her waist as he crushed her body to his and found her mouth.

Relief pulsed through her. This was no ghost. He was real! He bruised her mouth with his force. All the while her heart was singing, *He's alive! Dios! He's alive!*

When he finally released her, she gasped in air. "I thought you were dead!"

His blue eyes burned into hers. "Don't you know I'm too mean to kill?"

When she didn't smile, but gave up a hiccupy sob, he leaned down, cupped her chin in his hand and kissed her cheeks. "It is all right, Victoria," he said seriously. "See? Touch me. I'm here." He pulled her hand to his chest where she felt the wild beating of his heart.

She trembled as she reached for his face and stroked his jaw, so rough with whiskers. Did he understand how she'd blamed herself for his being at the Alamo? Even when he'd claimed not to care about Tejas, he'd stayed to be slaughtered.

And now he was here.

"How did you do it? How did you escape?"

He pulled back. "Slipped over the wall. Hid in the brush by the lake."

"During the battle?"

He hesitated, his eyes narrowing slightly. "You know it is over then?"

"I have not heard the cannon for two days. It is silent now," she said.

Jake expelled a breath. "Of course. You would know, then."

"But when did you leave?"

A furrow formed between his brows as he met her gaze. "Before the attack. The night of your departure."

So he'd left the others to their fate. A fate he would have shared had he stayed. She saw the uncertainty in his eyes—the yearning for acceptance of his actions. Could she give it? He waited to see how she would judge him.

"I would have stayed to protect you but when you were no longer there it didn't make sense any longer. Once I was free of the Mexican encampment I knew you were safer with Diego than with an Anglo. If you didn't need me, then I needed to find my brother."

"And did you find him?"

He explained about going to Gonzales and learning the truth of Brandon from Juan, about his decision to come back for her instead of continuing on to Goliad. And then seeing the smoke from the fires.

In her heart, she understood his words. It was her mind that rebelled against them. She curled her fingers into fists, wanting to hate him. "All those men—they needed you, but I could not bear it if you had died!" she said softly, feeling the shift inside her—the part of her that demanded perfection in everything and everyone. Life was not perfect, as he'd said. It was not always black-and-white. People usually did the best they could.

"I'm not a hero, Victoria. You knew that from the start. I'm just a man."

She took in a shuddering breath. "I have no right to judge you. I left, too, didn't I? After all my prideful talk, we are the same."

Slowly he reached out and touched her cheek. "No. Never that."

The look in his eyes had her catching her breath. It spoke of acceptance and something else—something more.

She leaned against his hand, closing her eyes to enjoy the feel of it on her. It was so hard to think clearly when all she wanted was to feel his touch, know his kiss again. Yet before any more was said, she had to warn him about the soldiers. They still watched the cabin and they would kill him on sight should they find him here. "You aren't safe here. You must go."

"I love you, Victoria."

Her breathing stopped.

"I understand there can be nothing between us— you being such a lady. I just want you to know that I am here for you. To do whatever I can to help you through this—for as long as it takes until you are back on your own land."

Overcome, she could only stare up at him. "You came back, for me?" Thinking of the danger he'd faced humbled her. "Jake, you risk too much. The Santanistas—"

He stopped her words. "I had to know that you were safe and that I hadn't ruined everything. God, Victoria—I'm sorry. I should have been here."

"It's all right. You thought I would be safe with

Diego when I left the fort, and I have been. Don't do this to yourself." His conscience was tearing him apart. She kissed his jaw, then pulled his mouth to hers for another kiss. "You can't change how I feel about you, Jake. It is impossible."

His throat worked as he swallowed hard. "Victoria, I'm trying my damnedest to keep from bedding you. You are not making this easy." He drew in a deep breath. "I told myself I'd be content to find you alive and unharmed."

She drew back, frowning. "Like a doll on a shelf?"

"Like a woman destined for a better future than me."

Anger flared. How dare he say such a thing! Was his love so weak? Where was the confident, cavalier Anglo she'd first known? The one who had captured her heart with his bold teasing and audacity, her brave *caballero*.

Searching his face, she knew he hadn't changed— not that part of him. He had revealed but another part of who he was—the part he hid from the world. And now he would deny his desires to honor her. This was not the mark of a cad, but the essence of a noble man.

She'd always made it clear she was higher born than he, better than he. She had never given him reason to expect otherwise. None of that mattered now. She wanted to give him something of herself, something precious. Something she could give to no other man. He already had her heart....

She closed her mind to the voices of her ancestors and slowly raised her hands to his face. "But I don't want another. I want only you."

"It will ruin you," he whispered, his voice hoarse, but his lips grazed hers, his warm breath stirring the air between them.

"You did that with your first kiss," she admitted. "I am already yours."

Raw desire flared in his eyes before he lifted her into his arms and kissed her firmly, claiming her as his, the decision made. His eyes were so blue—bluer than she'd remembered. He smelled of pine trees and his own mixture of sweat and leather.

He tumbled her onto the bed, landing on top of her, supporting his body with his arms so as not to crush her. His mouth hovered inches from her own. His whiskers rubbed against her cheek and she felt a glorious burn. He had come back to her! She tugged at his shirt, yearning to feel the warmth of his skin against hers.

He grabbed her hand. "Slow down. We've got all night."

"You are talking too much, *señor*," she teased, daring him. "I am not a patient woman."

His eyes turned serious. "But this is your first time."

"That doesn't mean I'll break if you move a little faster."

"Sometimes faster is not better," he said, and unbuttoned his shirt. She spread open the edges, revealing dark-brown hair sprinkled across his chest. She ran her hand over him, and pleasure uncoiled deep inside.

"Lower." His gaze never left hers.

Slowly, she moved her hand lower, drifting lightly over his naval and then the tapering of his waist. His abdominal muscles tensed.

He sucked in a breath.

"Lower," he said again.

She stilled, the only sound she heard was her pulse pounding in her head. "Jake…"

"Lower." His blue eyes burned into hers, daring her further.

Her heart beat rapidly as she dipped her hand beneath his belt and skimmed along his skin, moving toward his back and the curve of his spine. Her hand was cool compared to the heat that radiated from him, his muscles firm under her touch. Slower now, she slid to his front again. A bulge there stopped her from going farther. She didn't remove her hand.

Jake's eyes closed then and he trembled. That she could elicit such a response by a mere touch filled her with a deep satisfaction. A power was here that she had not known of before. A power to respect.

He opened his eyes, his breathing ragged as he promised, "Your turn, *señorita.*"

He untied her hair ribbon, letting it drop to the bed, and then ran his fingers through her hair. He leaned in to nuzzle below her ear, his warm breath sending tingles across her skin and breasts. Unbuttoning her blouse, he pushed it from her shoulders, stopping to drop kisses on the bare skin he'd exposed.

"Jake…" she whispered as she felt the tension inside her coil.

"Shhh. Too much talking, remember?"

"But…"

He moved over her to kiss her thoroughly. "Shhh…"

"I…I'm cold. I'm shivering."

"That's not from the cold."

She thought he smiled as he undid her camisole ribbon and pushed the cotton material to her waist. His assurance didn't make her feel any better. "How would you know?" But she knew. It was because he'd been with other women. He was not the white knight of a young girl's dreams, but a man, flesh and blood, who had truly lived life.

His smile was mysterious. "Because I feel the same way, too."

"Oh."

"Come here. I'll warm you." He removed her blouse and skirt, tossing them across the bed. His clothes quickly followed, becoming part of the same heap and falling to the floor.

Her breath caught as he glided down the length of her, skin to skin, and pulled the covers over them. Never had she felt anything so heavenly and so earthy at the same time.

He took one breast in his hand, kneading it, and lowered his lips to her. She would have to modify her previous thought. This…this was even more sensation than she could handle.

"Are you warm now?" he asked, his whiskers tickling her skin.

A long, low moan escaped her, and she felt a drawing in her center.

"You are so soft, Victoria. Soft where I am hard."

Another shiver coursed through her at his words.

"Touch me, too, Victoria," he urged. "Hold me."

Thrilled and a little nervous, she moved her hand along his torso, dipping to hold the curve of his buttock and then sliding around in front to hold him.

She turned to kiss his neck, his cheeks, his lips again. A yearning gripped her and she deepened her kiss, pressing her body against his, demanding more from him—and still she was not close enough. His hand skimmed her flat stomach, caressing, and moved lower to slide between her legs.

"Jake…" She tensed, her entire body throbbing.

"I love you," he said and kissed her hard. His tongue plunged into her mouth as he entered her below.

A burning sensation ripped through her center. She stiffened and cried out, the sound swallowed deep inside his mouth. She closed her eyes, grateful that he was still.

After a moment she felt a shuddering breath go through him. "The first time is not easy on a woman."

"It doesn't hurt. Not really," she lied.

He kissed the tears from her eyes. "It will go easier now. I promise." He started to move, slowly, carefully.

And she found he was right. Hesitantly, she joined in with the rocking motion of his body and realized the pain slipped away, replaced by waves of pleasure. The sensation grew, and she found herself straining to take in more of him. She arched her back and he slipped his arms around her to hold her tight against him, her breasts rubbing against his warm chest.

The rhythm built, coursing through her. Her world narrowed to the one-room cabin, the firelight glowing on his shoulder, the feel of his skin warm against hers and the love she felt for him.

"Look at me, Victoria. I want to see you."

She focused on his face floating above her, glazed with love and a reverence she'd not seen before. He wrapped his arms around her shoulders, and with a final growl, he spilled himself into her.

"*Te quiero,* Jake Dumont," she said softly, and held him until she felt his body relax.

He moved to her side, cocooning her in his warmth, her backside flush against him. He kissed her neck and then whispered in her ear, "Apart from the rifle pointed at my chest, that was the best welcome I've ever had."

Jake woke at first light. A rooster crowed in the distance. Pale daylight filtered around the edges of the dark covers over the windows. In front of him, Victoria lay curved into his body, a warm remembrance of the night before. He pushed a wisp of hair from her cheek, marveling at the silkiness of the strand.

Last night had been more than he'd ever thought possible. Victoria had dropped all her defenses and opened up to him—vibrant and alive, taking what she needed and giving back at the same time. She had become his in all ways. And she'd told him she loved him, giving him the most precious gift a woman can give—her virginity. Could he begin to hope for a future with her?

He sighed. Some men seemed to have women that stood by them, but not the Dumonts. It didn't run in their makeup. His mom had taken off. And look what Caroline had done to Brandon. Hadn't his father always said not to trust them? Enjoy them, use them, but never promise them anything. And above all, never let yourself fall for them.

Just one more thing he would disappoint his father on. He'd fallen for Victoria in a long, fatal plunge from the moment he'd set eyes on her. It scared the living daylights out of him how much he cared for her.

He'd do the right thing by her if she would have him. He wasn't a blue blood by any stretch of the imagination, and he couldn't believe she would ever want him in her life permanently. He didn't fit. Not for things like children and happily-ever-after. But he would hang on as long as she'd have him, as long as he could protect her and make her happy.

He looked down the length of her body, taking in the curves that had driven him wild during the night. They still drove him wild, but he needed to wake her. They had to put as much distance between themselves and the Mexican soldiers as possible today. Throughout the night he'd felt the urgency building.

He planted a kiss on her exposed shoulder, noting the redness. Similar areas blotched her cheeks and the top of her breasts. He rubbed the whiskers on his jaw. So rough. It was a wonder he hadn't rubbed her skin right off.

Well, that was one thing he could make short work of. He slipped from the bed and strode to the window to check the position of the sun. Hopefully not much daylight had passed. And where was Diego? The boy seemed to have melted discreetly away last night. Jake would have to thank him for that someday.

"Where are you going?" Victoria asked from the bed. Tousled and sleepy, she rose on her elbow.

It took all his strength not to climb right back in and take her again. "I've scrubbed you raw with my whiskers. Time to shave. I'll be more careful about that from now on."

"Oh."

She sounded disappointed. A fact that had him beaming on the inside. "And we have to leave. I'll feed and saddle the horses and wake up Diego if he's in the barn. He's probably cursing us for locking him out in the cold."

She sat up quickly, leaving the bed and pulling on her clothes. "Before you go, Jake, there is something I must tell you."

He grunted. If only she could read his thoughts. Talking was the last thing on his mind. "There'll be time enough when we hit the trail. I want to get you somewhere safer than this."

He wanted to banish that serious look from her eyes. The one that said they had to figure everything out this minute. He also wanted to reassure her that he wasn't leaving her—that he wasn't just taking the gift she'd given and running.

"About last night," he began. "I'll stand by you, Victoria. Whatever you want—however far you want to take this."

A smile crossed her face, breathtaking in its trust and simple beauty.

Feeling relieved and content all at once, he slid his hat on his head. "I'm anxious for a repeat performance."

He strode to the door and grabbed his rifle, glancing back once more to make sure he'd brought the sparkle back to her eyes, and then walked outside.

The horses stood in the small barn, but Diego was nowhere to be found. An indentation in the straw indicated where he'd slept. Maybe he'd gone to the creek to wash up. Jake fed and watered the horses, amazed to see a small supply of oats set aside that they could eat. He stepped outside.

And froze midstep.

Chapter Fourteen

"*Hola, Señor.* Please drop your rifle."

Twenty soldiers, ten on horseback, formed a half circle around him. The one who'd spoken sat his horse arrogantly and wore a tall, feathered hat and pompous uniform. He was the one in command, Jake surmised and gripped his rifle all the harder. At the moment it was his only means of defense.

Two soldiers stood nearby and held the horses that had been released from the hacienda's corral the night before. Had they been searching for the mounts and come upon this shelter? Jake cursed under his breath. Just his luck.

He thought briefly of ducking back into the barn, but realized the futility of it. Besides, he couldn't warn Victoria if he did that. He glanced toward the cabin and saw that the door was open wide. Had Victoria been smarter than him? Had she heard the soldiers approach and hidden in time?

His answer came when he heard scuffling inside the cabin and then a shriek. Something crashed against the wall, and the sound of breaking glass reached his ears. God, he felt so helpless. How could he help her?

"Your rifle, sir. Now."

He stared down the man and slowly lowered his gun to the dirt. "I hope the great Santa Anna does not make war on women."

A slow smile spread over the face of the Mexican officer, curling the edges of his thin mustache. "I am General Cos, *señor.* And of course we do not harm women, misguided as they are regarding this war."

A muffled cry came from the cabin. A soldier shoved Victoria through the door, his hand covering her mouth. Her eyes widened in alarm when she saw Jake, and she struggled against the man who held her.

His heart knocked wildly in his chest. She needed him. He started toward her.

A sword sliced the wind and blocked his path.

"Señor," said the general, "you will not live to know what happens to her, but your actions could impact things greatly. *Entiendes?*"

Jake glared at him. There had to be something he could do!

An officer emerged from the cabin and spoke in low tones to the soldier manhandling Victoria. Victoria struggled against her assailant, but then, after hearing the officer's words, suddenly stopped. The foot soldier released her and stepped away. Then he did something that surprised Jake further—

He bowed to her!

Confounded, Jake watched as the soldier motioned to two others to follow him into the barn.

Jake kept his eyes trained on the man with Victoria. When the officer stepped off the porch and into the sunlight, Jake felt like he'd been gut-punched. It was the man from the kitchen—her former suitor—Esteban.

Hope bubbled up. Perhaps Victoria would pull free of this after all. She claimed that Esteban was her friend. Perhaps that meant he still felt friendship toward her despite her siding with the rebels. Jake didn't care about himself. He figured he didn't stand a chance. Santa Anna took no prisoners. But if Victoria could survive this…

"General Cos," Esteban said for the benefit of all. "This woman has proven her worth to us. She has kept the enemy busy until we arrived."

No response came from the general.

"We owe her a debt of gratitude. Not ill treatment."

"I will determine that," General Cos barked. "This is not Juan Seguín. You promised me Seguín."

"No. But we have word of his position now."

Jake's thoughts reeled. Esteban's words couldn't be true! He looked at Victoria, saw her lift her head high and look away from him. A sinking sensation in his stomach made him nauseous. After all this time with her it couldn't be that his first impression of her was true! Had she deceived him all along?

If so, she was very good at her game. She'd played

him like a fool, made him believe that it was for him she'd left the Alamo when all she'd wanted to do was get word to the enemy of the dire straits of the men inside the walls. Of the fact, perhaps, that Juan had been ordered to leave and gather reinforcements and so would not be there at the final slaughter. Cold anger began to burn inside him.

Had last night been just that? A way to hold him until the soldiers arrived? He could hardly believe she'd go to that extreme, but then, he really didn't know her all that well. What had she said when he opened the door?

I was expecting Juan.

She must have been waiting for Jake to show up all along. Her playacting had been perfect. Perfectly evil.

And what of Diego? He was suspiciously absent this morning. And last night—the realization stung Jake—he'd acted strangely. The second Jake had told him Juan was on his way back to Gonzales, Diego had relented and brought him to Victoria.

He felt as if the wind had been sucked from his lungs. A fool. He'd been a damn fool and he'd walked into it with his eyes wide open. His muscles tensed. He wanted to hit something, preferably Esteban.

Behind him, two horses were led from the barn. The soldiers had saddled them. One soldier was busy rifling through Brandon's medical bag.

It was the last straw. It was all Jake had left of his brother and he'd be damned if he let the Mexicans take it. He let out a roar and lunged into the soldier, surprising him and knocking him down. His fist rammed into the man's face and blood gushed from his mouth as he bit down on his tongue. Jake ripped the bag from his hands.

"Retene!" the general ordered.

Two soldiers grappled for Jake, caught his arms and pulled him off the bloodied one on the ground. Quickly the man scrambled to his feet, holding his jaw and cursing. As the others held Jake back, he stepped forward and spit blood on Jake's face.

"What is it you have there?" General Cos demanded, motioning for the bag to be brought to him. He rummaged through it, examining the instruments and jars.

He looked at Jake. "This is yours?"

"Yes." He didn't figure Brandon was any of the man's business.

"Usted es médico?"

Unsure of what the general said, Jake remained silent.

General Cos regarded him disdainfully. "You will come with us." He gave the bag back to the soldier with instructions to pack it.

Jake found his hands tied and the rope looped around the saddle horn of one of the horses. Then he was shoved up on his horse.

He glanced at Victoria. She stood on the porch, her face rigid. Esteban stood close behind her. He moved closer, his mouth to her ear as though he were breathing in her scent.

Jake's gut twisted.

The traitors. They'd planned this from the start and he'd gotten in their way. She'd betrayed him in the worst way. All her claims of loyalty and doing what needed to be done were lies… Like the mist they had no substance.

Like her, too.

He would never forgive her. He'd been right from the start. Never trust a woman. He wouldn't make the same mistake again.

Victoria watched as Jake was led away on his horse. His dark look frightened her, piercing through to her heart. He wanted her dead. A chill swept over her. She felt the brunt of Esteban's pistol at her back.

"A moment more, Señorita Torrez," he whispered in her ear.

She waited, fighting the overwhelming urge to break and run to Jake. She loved him. Completely. A future without him would be unbearable.

And he thought she had betrayed him.

Esteban held the gun on her while all the soldiers departed, swallowed up by the cover of the trees. Still Victoria waited and tried to control her body's urge to shake. *Respire,* she told herself. *Just breathe.* She wanted to be strong. She would be strong if she could just block the fear inside.

Esteban was not the same man who had helped her escape from Laredo, of that she was certain. He had changed for the worse.

She trembled again.

"You may relax now, *señorita.*"

"I will, when you move that *pistola* from my back." She tried to keep her voice firm and strong, but even she could hear how weak she sounded.

"Still wanting your own way. When will you learn? As I said once before, your father was too lenient."

Esteban motioned to the *soldados* beside him. "Wait here."

"*Capitán—*" One looked her over, a leer breaking on his face.

Esteban silenced him with a glare.

The grin on the junior officer's face was replaced with one more shuttered.

Esteban took her arm and shoved her inside the cabin, slamming the door shut behind him. He did not lower the gun. Instead he slowly trailed the end of it along her waist, up between her breasts, pausing a moment over her heart. His eyes took on the hard look of slate. "You did well. But I wanted Seguín— not the Americano. He is nothing to me." He circled around her and then glanced at the tousled bed.

She swallowed hard. "I did as you asked."

His eyes flashed back at her. "I told you. Seguín is the reason you were allowed to stay and Diego was allowed to live. General Santa Anna wants Seguín's head as an example to the men of Mexico."

"Juan is too smart to be caught."

"What did your *amor* have to say about him? And do not think to lie to me," Esteban taunted. "Remember I have Diego, and I would not be afraid to demonstrate how much I expect the truth."

Victoria's chest tightened. She did not for one moment believe that Diego would hand over Juan, but what had he told Esteban?

"Now tell me—what of Seguín?" Esteban pressed.

"Juan is…" She stopped, not knowing what to say. Juan had a good day-and-a-half start on Esteban, but still she didn't want to give his position away.

"Go on." Esteban's eyes narrowed on her.

She felt her resolve start to crumble. "You promised that Diego would go free," she reminded him.

Esteban raised his brows. "You haven't told me anything yet."

She took a deep breath and met his eyes. "Juan is on his way to the town of Mina. Now let Diego go. He is nothing to you."

He studied her. "This war has changed you, Victoria. But not so much that I still can't tell when you lie."

"What do you mean? I've done everything you asked! You said you would let Diego go!"

"Not yet. First we will find out who lied. Diego gave us another destination for your cousin. General Cos will send out soldiers in both directions. Then we will see," he taunted her. "We will see. You will both come with me."

Victoria froze. *Go with him?*

Esteban's smile was cold as he moved to the bed and drew back the covers. A smear of blood marked the coarse sheets. "I wanted you, too. But now—now I am not so sure. You gave yourself cheaply, Victoria.

To a Norte Americano. Was it worth it? He will live only as long as he is useful to Santa Anna."

She closed her eyes against his cruel words, her heart aching.

Esteban opened the door and said a few words to the two soldiers outside. He tore her cloak from the wall peg and as they stepped off the porch he turned and threw it over her shoulders. "Don't worry further about the Americano. He believes you are mine now."

A keening cry sprang from her chest as she sank to the floor. She buried her face in her hands. It was true. Jake's last glance, filled with hate, had confirmed it.

A vicelike hand gripped her arm as Esteban forced her to her feet and dragged her outside. The cold wind numbed her face as he forced her up on a waiting horse and tied her hands together over the saddle horn. It didn't matter. Her heart was already numb. Jake would loathe her forever.

Jake couldn't figure out why General Cos hadn't plugged him the moment he saw him. It had to have had something to do with the medical bag. The contingent joined the rest of the troops at Juan's hacienda for the trek to Béxar, and then they met thousands more as they arrived. Stares and jeers followed him as the dragoons led him on horseback through the streets.

The first thing he noticed was the large number of buzzards circling overhead. They took turns swooping down to disappear below the line of trees at the river. As the contingent passed the walls of the Alamo, Jake averted his eyes. Too many men he knew had fought and died there. With a heavy heart he kept his gaze on the path before him, on the rump of the horse that walked in front of his—anything but those walls.

As they marched near the bridge into town. Jake followed the flight of a buzzard to the river and saw the bodies of Mexicans and Texians alike scattered in grotesque disarray in the water and on the river's bank. Overwhelmed, he doubled over on his horse and retched. A stream of Spanish curses chased him as the soldiers behind him sidestepped his vomit.

Though small, the feeling of revenge felt sweet.

They took him to a stately home on the corner of the Main Plaza and waited while General Cos dismounted and stepped inside. A moment later General Santa Anna strode through the open door.

So this was the president of Mexico. One who, with an army of thousands, would crush a handful of dissenters for daring to expect his protection and the keeping of promises he'd given years ago. A man without the capacity of compassion. A man without a heart.

With a careless glance at Jake, Santa Anna motioned for Brandon's bag. A soldier removed it from his pack and handed it over. After a cursory examination of the contents, the general tossed it back and walked inside his house followed by Cos.

A soldier ordered Jake to dismount. With hands

still roped and tied, he was pushed across the street to a small house. Inside, the soldier shoved him down with his back against the interior wall of the house. Apparently, this is where he was to stay until they decided what they were going to do with him. Whatever was to happen, at least he had not been killed yet, which meant he might have a chance to escape.

The next day a woman brought him beans wrapped in a tortilla to eat and a gourd of water. Afterward a soldier took him outside to relieve himself and then escorted him to another house down the street. Men lay sprawled in varying positions around the room, a few on pallets, but most on the dirt floor.

The soldier shoved him down on his knees before the first man. The prone Mexican looked at him suspiciously. *"El médico,"* the soldier beside him said.

Jake started to rise.

A hand clamped on his shoulder and shoved him back down, hard. The man on the ground cautiously raised his dirty shirt, revealing a bloody wad of cloth the size of his fist against his waist. Jake met the injured man's gaze.

Apparently they took him for a doctor.

All right. If this would keep him alive awhile, he'd do what he could. He thought about the few remedies he knew from watching his father as a boy. He'd learned a few things on his own and from other hunters and scouts he'd run into. He'd seen boils lanced, snakebites handled—maybe he knew enough to fool the Santanistas. It wouldn't be much, he realized, looking around for bandages and supplies and seeing none at hand. Whatever he did, he'd just better make it look authentic. If they found out he knew nothing about medicine, he was dead.

The makeshift bandage caked with dried blood had been pressed to the wound, probably for days. If he removed the bandage, the scab could pull off and the blood might start flowing again. Then what would he do?

Jake motioned to the soldier beside him. "Get me water and my bag."

The man didn't understand him.

"*Agua.* My bag. *Médico.*" He made the motions of pouring water and lifting a bag at the same time that he spoke, wondering if he'd come close at all to saying the words correctly.

The soldier gave orders to another man. Jake listened hard. If it meant staying alive, he'd learn their damn language. He would learn as much as he could about the enemy. And he'd wait for a chance to escape. When he did get away, he'd circle back and give that lying Victoria a taste of her own medicine.

Chapter Fifteen

The sun rose distant and cold on the sixth day of his captivity. After leaving a brace of soldiers behind to control the town, Santa Anna had left Béxar to march the rest of his army to Goliad. They'd camped beside the San Antonio River at night and followed the river south during the day. Jake looked constantly for a chance to escape, but the soldiers that guarded him were deathly afraid of the vengeance of President Santa Anna should they fail in their duty.

The president, Jake observed, was as strict and cruel to his own forces as he was to the enemy. While he sat in luxury in his tent with a mistress to engage him, food and drink from china plates, and a personal musician to keep him entertained, the men in his army had to make do with very little. Despite the uniforms they wore, many had no shoes but wrapped their feet in rags. Jake figured their shoes had worn out on the march north from Mexico City and since they only had one pair, they had to do the best they could. He also saw boots on some that looked as if they'd been taken from the men at the Alamo. It was a sight that filled him with ambivalence. With Santa Anna insisting they march through the winter, they'd had small rations and only the food they could take from a barn here or there, or livestock from a place such as Victoria's.

The march had been hard on all of them. Jake could see it in their bony wrists and, when they happened to grin, in the absence of a tooth here and there. They bore his ministrations in silence and suspicion, ever watchful. He'd heard countless prayers offered to St. Jude as infection had set in on many of the wounds. He just thanked God that he wasn't accused of killing the ones that had died. They would have died, anyway.

He leaned over the river and soaked a cloth in the icy water, runoff from the snow high in the mountains. When he returned to his campsite, the woman who had been bringing him food for the past week was waiting. He nodded to her and took the corn paste she offered in a bowl and the cup of muddy water. While he ate, she kept up a stream of rapid conversation with the soldier that stood guard over him. She stamped her foot on the hard ground and her voice increased in volume.

When he'd finished eating, he handed back the bowl and cup. *"Gracias."*

The soldier nudged him with his rifle and indicated he was to follow the woman. He wiped his hands on the wet cloth again and draped it over a rock to dry. As he turned to fall in step behind the woman, the soldier pushed Brandon's medical bag at him. Apparently there were more wounded to be seen.

The size of the camp was staggering. He walked around tents strung between trees, fire pits, and clothes draped over lines to dry in the brisk breeze. Some men were already up and packed for the day's trek. He reached the edge of the encampment and found that those on the outskirts did not even have tents to protect them from the weather. Bedding lay strewn on the ground, with sacks of rags used for pillows and blankets tattered and worn through with holes. This area, he realized as he looked around, contained the camp followers—the wives and children and even the prostitutes of the soldiers. They were a bedraggled bunch and worn down. The march north had been much harder on them.

The woman led him to a campsite where another woman lay. A makeshift tarp of hide blocked the wind so that a small fire heated the area. Up to now he'd just attended to the soldiers. He had no idea how to help a woman.

The older woman grabbed his arm and pulled him down. The woman on the ground was beautiful, or had been before spending the winter in the field. Dark lashes lay against pale skin, reminding him briefly of Victoria. He crouched before her wondering what was wrong other than malnutrition.

"Carmen!" the older woman said sharply.

The eyes fluttered open and stared into his. No fear, no question as to why he was here. Nothing. They looked vacantly into his, staring and not seeing him. He wondered if she still had her mind. His gut twisted at the sight

"Carmen!" the woman said again, apparently disgusted that her friend wasn't moving. She kneeled down and pulled off the blanket, revealing the woman's shape, swollen with child.

Jake drew back. He knew nothing about childbirth. He swallowed hard. He couldn't do anything to help this woman.

He started to stand when the older woman pulled him back down and removed the blanket from the young woman's feet. Jake leaned closer to examine them. Crusted with blood and bruised beyond recognition, he wondered how she'd managed to walk as far as she had. Every step must have been excruciating. It was a wonder she hadn't lost the baby—not enough food, not enough rest, and pressed beyond her endurance.

Victoria's face came to mind. These two looked to be the same age, only Victoria had finer lines. He wet a rag in the bucket of lukewarm water sitting near the fire. He hoped he didn't make her injuries worse. Kneeling beside her, he picked up her foot and propped it on his thigh. She winced as the cold air breezed over her skin—or was it his touch that made her pull away?

He settled her foot again on his leg and began cleansing the cuts and scrapes. Methodically, he worked, going from the more superficial wounds and slowly working toward the deeper ones. The woman held herself stiff and seemed ready to bolt. He couldn't blame her. Why should she trust anything he did? In her place, he wouldn't.

Taking the jar of ointment from his bag, he smeared the last of it over the abrasions and wrapped her feet in rags the old woman handed him. "She must rest a day," he said.

His guard shook his head. "We go. *Vamanos.*"

Jake stood and faced him. "She needs to rest."

The guard ignored him. The old woman met Jake's gaze.

"Where is her husband?" Jake persisted. "He can stay behind one day, can't he?"

He didn't think the soldier would answer. A muscle in the man's jaw worked as he held his tongue. When he finally turned to Jake, his eyes filled with cold anger. "He is dead. You rebels killed him."

His words sent a shiver through Jake. The woman must hate him. He looked at her as she huddled in the thin blanket. How had she withstood his touch?

He picked up his medicine bag and headed back to his camp. There must be some way to help her. To leave her behind would be her death—and he'd seen too much of death. He stopped, meeting the dark gaze of the guard. "Then make a travois for her. My horse can pull it."

The soldier didn't move to help—did not even blink an awareness that Jake had spoken.

"He does not take orders from a prisoner," a familiar voice said from behind him, sending chills down his back. Esteban stepped into view from a nearby tent, speaking as he buttoned up his coat.

"So you've figured it out," he said. "You stay alive as long as you have value—to Santa Anna."

"A secure arrangement," Jake said sarcastically.

"For the moment you have proven to be a fairly good doctor. A surprise considering my first impression of you."

A surprise to Jake, too. He hadn't realized that so much of his father's examples had stayed with him.

"Have you nothing to say?" Esteban continued. "No grateful appreciation that you are still alive? It is more than your comrades got. I have wondered about that—how you escaped when they didn't."

Rage boiled up in Jake as his hand closed into a fist. Esteban's hand covered the hilt of his sword. "Think before you attack an officer, Señor Dumont. It will be your last breath."

"And I'll enjoy it."

Esteban's eyes turned steely, but he stood there, waiting, almost taunting Jake to carry out his threat.

The man had gone too far. What right did he have to judge Jake? Esteban had stood by and given the Texians no quarter, no mercy. Only a slaughter. It had been a bloodbath.

Jake hesitated. And *he'd* run.

He'd told himself it was because he needed to find Brandon, but was that really true? Esteban thought him a coward. Jake could see it in his eyes.

The captain glanced down at the woman and took in the situation. "El Presidente would not want us to slow our march because of her. She is nothing." His cold gaze returned to Jake in a blatant challenge to argue with him.

Jake clenched his fists. If this was how the Mexican president thought of his people, then Jake wanted no part of him. And if this Esteban, Victoria's friend, could be so callous about the woman, how would he treat Victoria?

The thought jolted him. Why should he care? Victoria had betrayed him in the worst way. The two deserved each other.

Jake stared at Esteban, and hate churned inside. The man was baiting him. He could see it in his eyes. He wanted him dead. The only way Jake would get out of this alive was if he used his head. He couldn't let himself be goaded. Jake corralled his thoughts back to the woman.

"She won't slow us down." He pointed with his chin at the structure behind the woman which blocked the wind. "A travois can be made easily enough from the lean-to."

Esteban's gaze didn't waver. "Then you make it. We leave in one hour."

Jake wanted to strangle this arrogant man to within an inch of his life. To think that Victoria was in league with him disgusted him. To think of Victoria at all brought a rage better left buried for good.

"I need a hatchet."

Esteban looked amused. "No tools."

Jake pressed his lips together. He'd do it himself then. He turned and yanked the tarp from the tree branch. He grabbed the branch and pulled with all his might, twisting and turning the slender wood until it finally cracked and gave way.

Esteban watched for a moment, and then said something to Jake's guard before striding to his tent. Jake stopped working long enough to see him throw back the tarp flap and enter. Just inside the opening was the silhouette of a woman watching him— *Victoria.*

She was here! And she was with Esteban—apparently willingly. Rage congealed in Jake's stomach into a hard, white-hot mass.

Three soldiers walked by and stopped to watch Jake work. They laughed and joked among themselves as he tore the makeshift shelter apart with his bare hands. It felt good to take his anger out on the wood. Good to imagine the branches as Esteban's arms and face.

He placed the tree branches parallel and, with a strip of leather, lashed the tarp's edge to them. His hands grew stiff and raw with the icy wind. When he was finished, he strode to the makeshift corral and saddled the Spanish mustang he'd been given to ride, surprised in a way when no one stopped him from walking off with the animal.

He returned to the woman's camp, attached the travois to the horse and stepped over to the young woman. Around him, he noticed men striking camp and preparing to leave. He carried the woman to the travois. Laying her down, he covered her with her thin blanket and then mounted his horse. Somehow he'd get out of this mess. But for today—today he'd have to keep an eye on the woman. Soon he'd figure out a way to escape. Escape or die trying.

The march to the town of Goliad took ten days. Ten days of following the San Antonio River as it meandered toward the Gulf of Mexico. He never saw the pregnant woman again after that day and wondered about her. Had she survived the march? Had her injuries healed? Or had his work been for naught?

They forded the river a mile from Goliad and entered the town in the evening. On the southern bank and near the village, a mission and chapel stood. Across the river the Spanish Presidio stood alone, its massive stone walls towering over the flat Mexican plain. Jake looked around at the adobe houses and wooden buildings as he mentally mapped out the town. He'd need to be familiar with its layout if he escaped under cover of darkness.

He followed his guard to a latrine dug behind a house. From there, the cold metal barrel of a musket prodded him toward another house. He stumbled up the step and then righted himself before the guard marched him inside. A bowl of barely cooked beef was thrust into his hands. He ate quickly, greedily. The bowl was whipped from him before he could finish.

Looking around the room, he found men lying on pallets of straw. All Santanistas. Their bandages and positioning spoke of injuries in different stages of healing. The odor spoke of decay.

"No moverse." Stay. A candle flickered as the guard shut the door. Jake's legs ached from the forced march of the past five days. He'd had to walk. The mustang had been given to another soldier. His belly felt as if it was touching his spine in spite of the meat he'd just eaten—meat that was now trying to come back up. He drew his neckerchief over his nose to mask the pungent smell as he found an open spot on the ground to rest.

His days were filled with conjuring up plans of escape and caring for the injured Mexican soldiers. They confiscated the supply of bandages and the instruments that had originally been in the bag.

He kept his ears open, hoping to learn of Santa Anna's next move through the mutterings of the sick or the subdued conversations of the soldiers that stood guard over him. He learned that here in Goliad, General Fannin and his men had been taken prisoner by the Mexicans but were still alive. Jake wondered where they were housed. More than once he thought of Juan and hoped he had made it back to General Houston. When Jake escaped, if he escaped, he'd head that way, too.

No sense worrying about Victoria. Wherever she was in this town, Esteban now took care of her. The thought left a hollow feeling in Jake's gut.

Even when he was dead tired, lying on his pallet at night, he could not banish thoughts of her from his mind. She seduced him. Bewitching dreams of her teased and tortured him until he couldn't sleep. He would think of the soft line of her back, the silken skin of her shoulder that shone gold in the firelight, her teasing dark eyes, and he'd grow hard with wanting her. He could hate his body for that betrayal. Almost as much as he hated her for betraying him.

Almost.

On the tenth day, a soldier ferried him to the fort. In a small room more of the injured lay on the filthy floor. These men were different. They wore home-spun clothes. Were these Texians?

He bent over the first man. His face was black-ened with powder burns, along with his hands. Blistered skin extended to his elbows. The man moaned with the pain. Glancing around, Jake found nothing he could work with—no bandages, no medicine. The Santanistas had kept it all for themselves.

A bucket sat in the corner. Jake rose to his feet and grabbed it up. The guard at the door came in-stantly alert.

"I'm going to the river," Jake said. "These men could use a drink."

The guard apparently understood a few words, and nodded to another soldier to follow. Jake filled the bucket with the river water, taking a good look at the water level, the steep banks and the large rocks along them—rocks that might hide a man. Then he turned back to the fort.

Once inside, Jake took the bucket around to each man, pouring the water slowly into each mouth. Parched tongues, cracked lips—it looked as if they hadn't had water in days. He moved to the last man along the wall.

He appeared to be sleeping, or perhaps he was unconscious. He lay on his side, his arm thrown over his face. Dirty, oily brown hair flared over the wadded-up coat used as a pillow on the dirt floor. At first Jake saw no obvious injuries, no evidence of bleeding or powder burns.

"Soldier. Wake up. I've got water for you." He took hold of the man's shoulder and hip and rolled him over to his back.

An angry groan followed, and then a curse as the man curled up to brace himself on his elbows and wiped his face.

Jake's breath whooshed out of him.

Brandon!

My God! He'd found Brandon!

Chapter Sixteen

His brother's eyes opened wide as he recognized Jake in the same moment. "What the hell? Ja—"

With a look, Jake shook his head, warning Brandon not to give away the fact that they knew each other. His eyes stung, and his vision blurred as he held up the bucket. "Water," he said gruffly. "Take it or leave it."

At Brandon's dawning comprehension and nod, Jake held the bucket over his brother and dribbled water carefully into his mouth. His hands shook and the drops splattered Brandon's face and shirt. Setting the bucket down, he struggled against an overwhelming urge to touch Brandon. Then, ignoring the warning he'd just given his brother, he drew in a shuddering breath and reached out and grasped his wrist. Solid. He felt solid. Jake closed his eyes. For a man who didn't pray much, his thoughts came dangerously close to a prayer of thanks. He hadn't realized until that moment how much he'd given up on finding his brother alive.

Clearing his head, he glanced around to the guard at the door. The man acted like nothing out of the ordinary was going on. Jake intended to keep it that way.

He cleared his throat. "What's the problem, soldier?"

Brandon's eyes narrowed into slits. "They've made you the new doctor? You'll find it difficult without supplies."

Jake glared his answer.

"My ankle."

Jake moved down to examine Brandon's legs. He noticed then, that one pant leg had a dark stain stiffening the fabric. He rolled up the cuff and carefully removed his brother's boot. Slits had been made down the side of the leather to allow for swelling. At Brandon's swift intake of breath from the pain, Jake slowed his movements. A caked mass of old blood surrounded his ankle. "How long has it been like this?"

"Two days."

Jake looked closer, searching for evidence of infection.

"How'd it happen?"

His brother's jaw clenched. "What do you care? And what the hell are you doing here?"

Jake frowned at him. "You'll get us both killed if you don't lower your voice. All they need is an excuse."

Brandon shut his mouth, but his eyes glowed with an angry fire. Finally he answered. "Got caught trying to escape. Took a bullet there."

"Is the plug out? I can't tell."

"It's out. I used my knife before they took it away."

Jake shuddered. Could he have done the same in Brandon's place? Probably. But it would have been difficult. A new respect took hold for his brother. "Move your toes," he commanded.

The swollen toes wiggled slightly. Jake set about cleaning the wound as best he could by wetting his neckerchief in the water. He had to figure out a way to immobilize the foot and leg until it healed. And to keep it elevated. He surveyed his options around the room.

"Looking for feather pillows?" Brandon's voice was ripe with sarcasm. He tilted his head.

Jake speared him with a glance while he removed his coat, wadded it up and set it under his brother's leg.

Moving on to the next soldier, Jake did what he could for the man. Without medicine, that wasn't much. The next man was only a boy—fifteen years old if he was a day. And the man lying next to him was already dead.

Jake motioned to the guard who walked over to the still form, kicked the legs of the man and seemed satisfied he was dead. He nodded to Jake, who hoisted the man over his shoulder and followed the guard. Outside he was instructed to dump the body in a cart and return to the fort.

He did as he was told, but instead of turning back to the fort, he bowed his head. The least he could do was say a few words over this man—words that might ease his way into the next life. Surprisingly, the soldier standing at his side removed his hat and crossed himself.

"Lord, watch over the soul of this poor man who gave his all. Comfort his family. Take him to a better life."

Then Jake ripped the man's woven shirt off his body, turned and headed back into the fort. Let the guard think what he would and try to stop him. Jake would take care of the living now.

He tore the cloth into strips and knelt by Brandon. "Let me know if I get this too tight." He started at the arch of his foot and, moving up, wrapped the cloth around his brother's ankle. It had to be firm, but not so tight as to impede the circulation.

Brandon watched his movements, his body tense. "Who taught you to do this?"

Jake worked a minute more, wrapping upward toward the knee. "You did. When Samson tangled with that badger and you fixed his leg. You were twelve or so, but you had the makings of a doctor even then."

"Didn't think you took it all in. Oof! Be careful!"

Jake knew he was hurting him, and yet he had to do this if his brother was to have any chance of walking again. He wadded his coat again to provide a higher support, stuffing it back again under his brother's injured leg.

Brandon eyed him warily when he was finished. "Didn't think I'd make it, did you? You thought I'd turn back at the first difficulty."

The words were closer to the truth than Jake cared to admit. Did it make any sense to dredge it all up now?

"You had to come after me."

Bitterness tinged his brother's voice. Jake didn't know how to answer him other than to tell the truth.

"Yeah. I thought you would fail. Thought I'd catch up to you within a day or two. Didn't think I'd have to track you all the way here to Texas territory. I was surprised you made it. Surprised again when you immediately asked for duty." He hesitated a moment before adding, "Proud, too. Damn proud."

He met Brandon's blue gaze, so like his own. "We'll talk later. I need to see to the others." He started to rise when Brandon stopped him with his hand.

"How did they come to think you're a doctor?"

"I had your medical bag when they caught me."

Brandon's lips twitched. "Father's old bag?"

"I thought it was yours. Thought you might need it eventually." Call it silly, but he'd wanted something of Brandon's, too. Anything. He indicated the guard. "They have it now."

His brother struggled into a sitting position with his back flush against the cold stone wall. "Can't do much doctorin' now—which is why they wanted me around, too. They feed us once a day if we're lucky. They'll end up putting a plug in me when they get ready to move on. I'm too much trouble."

"I won't let that happen," Jake pledged.

"Now who's the dreamer?" Brandon sighed. He pulled back his pant leg again. "See that pus oozing around the scab?"

Jake swallowed hard. He'd noticed.

"There'll be a red streak soon." Brandon's smile was bleak. "Look out for yourself, Jake. You've always been good at that and I'm already dead."

A vice clamped on Jake's chest. He'd just found his brother. He wasn't going to let him die. Not now. Not like this.

"You may get out of this yet," Brandon continued. "If you do, go back to Charleston. Take that inheritance you wanted and enjoy it. It won't do me any good now."

"That's not why I came after you. It's never been about the money. You're my brother."

Brandon stared at him in astonishment.

"Don't look so surprised," Jake said gruffly. He hadn't spoken to his brother so plainly for years. He readjusted his coat under Brandon's leg again, unable to hold his gaze with his throat thick with emotion. "Good. Then we understand each other. So you can quit talking like that."

"Take that pretty *señorita* with you. She said you might come today. I didn't believe her."

Jake glanced at him sharply. Victoria? Did she have something to do with this?

In shock, he barely noticed when someone shoved him with a foot and knocked him off balance. He sprawled over Brandon's legs, cringing inwardly when he heard Brandon's hiss of pain. The guard towered over him and motioned for him to move on with his musket. Jake met Brandon's eyes in silent communication. He wouldn't be leaving town without him.

The guard shoved him again—harder this time. He reached for the wall to steady himself, stood and moved on to the next man, all the while wondering why Victoria had done this. What was in it for her? Or was it her way of tormenting him even more?

Chapter Seventeen

Victoria paced the length of the small room that was her prison. From the window she stared out into the mist gathering over the river as night approached. Would Esteban agree to her request? She had no way of knowing. He'd already been gone over an hour.

The door creaked behind her, and Jake stepped into the room followed by Esteban. Her heart stopped in her chest.

She wanted to run to Jake, to hold him once more. Instead, she forced herself to serenely stand her ground. He'd lost weight, as they all had. The angular planes of his face stood out prominently now, only partially covered by his beard. Rawhide strips tied his wrists together in front of him.

Startled to find her in the room, his eyes took on a glint of steel as he assessed the riding skirt she now wore, the more serviceable clothes. His mouth clamped shut into a thin line before he moved his gaze back to Esteban.

He thought the worst of her. She knew he didn't understand and probably never would, but this had to be done, even knowing he hated her.

Esteban removed his hat. The tension in the room mounted. His fingers drummed on the hilt of his sword as he paced the small room, his gaze darting frequently to Jake. "I believe no introductions are necessary. We all know each other now."

Jake met her gaze again and then looked away in disgust.

"I have been ordered to march the Texian soldiers into the meadow tomorrow—approximately three hundred and forty men. They are to be executed before we march north." He pinned Jake with his gaze. "You, among them."

"Why are you telling me this?"

Esteban waved his words away. "I have my reasons." He cleared his throat. "They laid down their arms, surrendering honorably. However El Presidente Santa Anna has decided not to keep to the terms of their surrender. I…I am bound to carry out his orders."

A muscle in Jake's jaw worked convulsively, his hands clenching. "And this comes as a surprise after the Alamo?"

Victoria stepped forward. One wrong move, one wrong remark, and Esteban might change his mind. She couldn't let that happen. He hated Jake for what he'd done to her. "Jake. Please. Hear Esteban out. Your anger only makes this more difficult."

"To what? Kill me quickly?"

"No," Esteban said. "To get you out of here."

Jake froze. "Why?" he asked suspiciously.

Esteban snaked his arm possessively around her waist. "Consider it a present. I wish for you to be a memory to Victoria. Not one that is dead, but one that she knows has left her of his own accord for his own selfish reasons. I want her to come to hate you for what you have done to her."

Victoria struggled to withstand Esteban's touch. Jake looked at her with such hate in his eyes that her heart ached with it. Unable to bear it, she turned her face away. She had to get through this. She must— or he would never make it out of here alive.

"How do I know I can trust you?" Jake asked warily.

Victoria felt Esteban shift her closer, felt his fingers tighten on her waist. "You don't."

"My brother goes, too."

Victoria couldn't help meeting his gaze as joy filled her. He'd found Brandon! She'd held little hope that the young man was his brother when she saw him being ferried across the river. It was his eyes that had stopped her. They were so similar.

"Brother?" Esteban repeated. "No. This would make it too difficult." He turned to Victoria and stroked a finger down her cheek. "And you, my dear, what more do you have to bargain with?"

Victoria held his gaze, her eyes cool. This was a game to him, but she would let Esteban do anything if it meant Jake would escape. It did not matter what happened to her after that.

"Well?" Esteban said, waiting.

She felt Jake studying her. Perhaps one day he would make sense of all of this and not judge her too harshly.

"He is at the fort with the injured prisoners," Jake said, more cautiously now. "I'm not going without him."

She put her hand on Esteban's chest, shutting out Jake, concentrating on what had to be done. "My land. It is yours."

He gave her a condescending smile. "But that is mine already. As soon as Santa Anna quells this rebellion I will have the title. He has decreed it."

She felt the hope draining out of her. She had nothing left to bargain with but herself. He'd made it clear before that she was nothing to him, that he was disgusted with her. During the journey she'd stayed in his tent and he hadn't tried to touch her. There had been moments, though, where she thought he watched her when he didn't think she saw him. Moments he'd stared at her with longing. She leaned up to whisper in his ear.

"Then let me pleasure you, Esteban."

She felt him tense and then pull back to look at her. "Willingly?" he asked.

She nodded.

Esteban let go of her and paced the length of the room. After another sharp appraisal of Victoria, he stopped midstride and faced Jake. "Is he able to ride a horse?"

Hope entered Jake's eyes. "He's been injured. I saw him two days ago. But I'll carry him. I'll do anything to get him out of here—take his place if need be."

Esteban waved off his suggestions. "That is not to my interest. How do you know he is still there? Infection could have taken him by now."

Jake shook his head. "No. I would know. Somehow I would know. He isn't dead."

Esteban pulled on his hat and stopped in front of Victoria. "I make no promises," he said to her, smoothing his hand down her neck.

She raised her chin, keeping her sight firmly on him. "But you are an honorable man, Esteban. A man who keeps his word," she said, steeling herself against his touch.

He acknowledged her with a nod. "To a point. Just as you are an honorable woman."

Victoria kept her gaze on him even though her eyes filled with tears. Esteban's words were a slap in the face to her, and they both knew it.

He drew her to him, whispering in her ear. "I will be back, *querída*. And we will make up for lost time." He kissed her on her temple. Then he pointed his musket at Jake, indicating it was time to leave.

As Jake passed by he brushed close enough to ruffle her skirt, close enough for her to feel the heat of him one last time. It would take only a second to reach out and touch him, but that second could jeopardize the truce with Esteban and ruin everything. So in the end she remained still, her arms crossed clutching her waist, and watched Jake leave. At the door he hesitated and looked back once more, searching her face for a moment. She saw no hate then, only questions. Questions she would never be able to answer. He turned and left.

As the door shut, Victoria heard Esteban give orders to a soldier to guard her and keep her inside. She took a steadying breath. It was over. She'd done all she could do. The rest was out of her hands. She could only hope that Esteban would keep his word and Jake would go free.

Esteban kept his bayonet fixed between Jake's shoulder blades as they walked down to the ferry landing. Minutes that seemed to stretch to hours passed as they floated across the river and climbed up the steep embankment.

Inside the fort, Esteban gave orders to the guard who then let them search the room. If possible the room stank more than when Jake had been there before, reeking of urine and old blood. Holding the lantern up for illumination, Jake peered into the corner, finding Brandon in the same heap where he'd left him. As Jake neared with the light, his brother's eyes opened, glazed over and feverish.

Jake swallowed hard, steeling himself against the sight. His brother's lips were cracked and bleeding from lack of water and the dry air. His skin had shrunken until his cheekbones stood out in sharp relief against the rest of his face. It hurt to look at him.

"You came back." Disbelief was ripe in his brother's raspy voice.

Jake breathed a prayer of thanks that Brandon was still alive. Barely—but he'd take barely over dead anyday. He grabbed up his own coat from the dirt and shrugged into it. "Here, put yours on. And be quiet."

He helped him into the coat he'd been using as a blanket noting that heat radiated off him. Jake wrapped his arm around his middle and stood him up on his one good leg. The effort made Brandon shake violently and gulp in huge draughts of air— whether from the pain or from weakness, Jake couldn't be sure. Neither reason was good.

Together they made their way outside, with Esteban prodding them with the butt of his rifle whenever they slowed.

"This way," Esteban said, urging them toward the river.

Jake hesitated. "Back to town?" He'd thought they would head the opposite way.

"The guards are watching. Do not do anything to make them more suspicious than they already are." Esteban jabbed Jake's shoulder with his gun.

Pain exploded down his arm. "Enough!" he said, growing angry. "Just get me to a horse. My brother can't walk."

Esteban shook his head. "Impossible. It is too dangerous now with the moon out. Francita Alavez will hide you until midnight."

A woman? Oh, Jake liked this plan less and less.

Once they'd crossed the river, the Alavez house was not far. It worked in their favor that it was on the outskirts of town. A young, pretty woman opened the door and let them pass through, nodding to Esteban in recognition. "In back, *Capitán*. And then I would have a word with you."

Esteban nodded and took them to a darkened room, telling them to stay put. Other men were huddled in the room, sitting on the floor, against the walls. Most looked like Anglos but there were a few Tejanos. Jake counted eighteen for sure. Everyone was silent.

He helped Brandon down to the floor, and then palmed his forehead to check for a fever. His skin was on fire. If they got out of this alive it would be a miracle. The woman brought a weak soup of broth and beef for them all. He spooned some into his brother's mouth, becoming even more alarmed when Brandon coughed and sputtered at first, his throat unused to any liquid.

The fever rose higher and his breathing became shallow and rapid. He grew frustrated as he tugged the sleeve of his coat, trying to remove it. Jake helped pull it off and then eased him back against the wall. For a moment his eyes focused coherently on Jake.

"Get out, Jake. Get out while you still can."

"I'm not leaving without you, so toughen up. I promised Caroline I'd bring you back. I aim to keep that promise."

Suddenly Brandon started to shiver, his teeth chattering loud enough to be heard clear into the next room. Jake threw the coat back over him and added his own, wrapping his arm around him for good measure.

"Whatever happened to Samson, anyway?" Jake asked, hoping to get Brandon's mind on something else. "Remember how he always took off after Mrs. Tarrington's cat?"

"He died."

Great. Definitely not the angle he was hoping for. "You mean your doctorin' didn't heal him?"

A weak smile worked its way up Brandon's face. "Naw. He bothered that cat and me for another good eight years. But he was always your dog, Jake. He wasn't the same after you left. Nothing was the same."

Jake had a feeling Brandon was talking about more than the dog. He couldn't answer to that. It was in the past. But he could answer to what he wanted for the future, if Brandon would let him. As his brother's breathing quieted and he slipped into an exhausted sleep, Jake considered what his next step would be…*if* they got out of here alive.

He thought back to what had transpired in the house—when he'd come upon Victoria. He'd been livid at seeing her with Esteban, and then the man had pawed her right in front of him. She'd nuzzled him right back. Right in front of Jake! It took all his willpower not to grab the hilt of his sword and run Esteban through.

She'd made it possible for him to find Brandon. He was sure of that from the things he'd heard. And remembering more, he realized that there were deep shadows under her eyes. He'd been too upset to notice them at first. What was it that she'd said at the house? Something about a bargain—and her land hadn't been enough.

His blood ran cold.

Had she been as much a captive as he? He thought back to their stolen time in the cabin. She'd tried to tell him something then, but he'd been too anxious to get moving that morning to listen. And here she'd managed to talk Esteban into releasing him and his brother. What had she given in return?

The moon had disappeared behind the tall cottonwood trees along the river when the door opened once again. Señorita Alavez motioned to Jake. He helped his brother to his feet and they both followed her. Esteban waited outside.

"Keep to the shadows," Esteban ordered in a strong whisper. They followed, Jake practically dragging his brother down the steep embankment to the river and stopping in a thick stand of trees to catch his breath.

A rider, cloaked in darkness, drew near, holding the reins of two horses. With the help of Esteban, Jake pushed his brother onto the first mustang. He turned to the next horse and recognized Fury.

Stunned, he glanced again at the dark rider, trying to make out the features beneath the cloak. Black eyes flashed at him. Diego.

"Señor Dumont. Mount. You must leave now." Esteban hissed the words.

Jake threw his leg over Fury and gathered up his reins along with those of Brandon's horse. He stared at Esteban a moment, and wondered if he was heading into another trap. "This is not over."

An ugly smile coated Esteban's face. "You are wrong, Señor. You heard her. She stays willingly. Señorita Torrez is no longer your concern."

They followed the river, keeping to the cover of trees. A mile north of town, they found a place shallow enough to ford, where large rocks edged the banks of the river, some projecting out over the water, creating small alcoves underneath. Wading through the rushing water, Jake heard noises—voices. He reined the horses toward the darkest shadows of the rocks motioning for Diego to follow. Astride their horses, they huddled, waiting and listening, while a small patrol of Mexican soldiers rode by.

Jake sensed the tenseness emanating from Diego. Anger smoldered in his eyes.

"What is it?"

"You left her there—with him," Diego said through a tight jaw. "I would like to leave you here, Anglo, but then I would be no better than you. I would not have kept my word to her, either." His dark look deepened as he nudged his horse on.

Jake reached out and grabbed the reins of Diego's horse. "There was never a doubt in my mind I'd go back for her. But I need your help. Will you wait here with my brother?"

Diego thought for a moment. "No. It is too dangerous. We'll keep moving."

"Where will I meet you?"

"Follow the river. When the trees stop for a space of twenty rods, the bottom is sandy and there is a long sandbar. Turn north there. I'll find you."

Jake nodded and moved near Brandon. "I don't have time to explain things now, but you can trust Diego."

Brandon pushed himself to sit up in the saddle. "Jake, you won't be so lucky again. What can I do?"

Jake put a hand on Brandon's shoulder, humbled for a moment that even in his weakened state, his brother would seek to help him. "Just hold tight to that saddle horn and keep riding. And pray that Dame Fortune smiles on me this one last time."

"I can't stop you, can I?"

"There's no way in hell I'm leaving her there. I have to do this. I'll catch up to you."

"Be careful."

Jake pressed his knees to Fury's flank, urging him out into the current.

It wasn't long before he reached the edge of town. He moved his horse through the water until they were both hidden beneath a low-hanging branch. Tying the reins, Jake moved stealthily along the riverfront to the house where he'd last seen Victoria. A guard stood at the door. Victoria must still be inside—hopefully without Esteban.

He searched the ground along the embankment for stones. Finding several, he threw one hard across the yard. It landed against the packed dirt pathway that circled the house. The noise roused the guard.

Jake threw his second stone before the soldier could relax again. It thudded in the dirt much like the first one.

"Who's there!" Musket in hands, the guard walked cautiously toward the stones to investigate.

Jake snuck up behind him, yanked the soldier's pistol from his belt and dashed the butt of it against the man's skull. Before uttering the shout of warning on his lips, the man collapsed in a heap on the ground.

Jake tucked the pistol into his waistband and grabbed the man's rifle. He hurried to the door.

"Victoria?" he whispered as his eyes tried to make out the room's interior. He saw a form slumped over the room's only table.

"Jake?" Her voice slurred as she roused. "Jake! What are you doing here? You are supposed to be safely away!"

He strode toward her voice. "Where's Esteban?"

"He hasn't returned yet."

The fact that she was waiting for Esteban stung for a brief second. "We must go. Get your cloak."

He heard the swish of her skirt as she hurried to do as he asked. When she neared, he grabbed her arm and pulled her against his chest, breathing in her soft fragrance. "I can't stand that another man has held you this close," he whispered. The thought twisted his gut, even as he was overcome with the need to kiss her.

The door burst open behind him.

"Victoria?" Esteban called.

Jake moved silently to the edge of the room, knowing Esteban's eyes would not see him—yet.

Victoria hesitated in the shadows. "I'm here. Is it done?"

Esteban lowered his pistol and walked toward the sound of her voice. "*Sí.* The guard is gone from your door. Did you hear anything?"

Jake stepped up to Esteban's side and slammed the butt of his pistol against his head.

Esteban reacted, firing his gun before sinking to the floor. The shot sounded deafening in the quiet town.

"Are you all right?" Jake asked, scared that Victoria might have been hit.

"Oh, Jake, we'll never get out of here now!"

"We will!" he insisted. He grabbed her hand and led her outside toward the river. They edged along the bank, stopping and crouching for a moment when they saw a soldier running toward the house they had just left. He paused over the still form of the guard then shouted an alarm and raced into the house. Jake pulled Victoria along the shore to his horse. Boosting her into the saddle, he climbed on behind her. The soldier ran out of the house firing his rifle into the air. Jake dug his heels into Fury's flanks. At his command, the horse bounded away against the water current, crossed to the opposite side of the river and struggled up the steep embankment among the willow trees.

"Juego!" The shout arose behind them. Another shot was fired, shattering a branch to their left. Jake kept his head low, protecting Victoria, as he urged Fury faster. Perhaps it was because Fury knew his rider well and sought to please him. Perhaps it was because Dame Fortune had for once smiled on Jake. Or perhaps it was because the Mexican soldiers knew many more would die at sunrise. To let one lone horse with riders leave seemed permissible against

such a stark and bloodstained day. Jake only knew that it was a miracle they made it safely away.

They raced to the place where he'd separated from Diego and Brandon in the shadow of the large rock. He stopped to let Fury rest at the water's edge. No soldiers patrolled this time. All was quiet in the moon's waning hour before the dawn.

He cupped Victoria's chin with his hand, urging her to turn toward him. "Forgive me," he breathed. "I was a fool." He studied her face in the pale light and waited for her absolution.

In answer she leaned into him and lifted her lips to his.

His kiss was reverent, thankful. "We'll see our way clear of this, Victoria. But don't ever risk so much for me again."

"I had to try. I love you."

He didn't deserve the love she showered on him. He hadn't trusted her. From the beginning he hadn't trusted her down deep where it really mattered.

She drew back, a smile forming. "You found him," she said. "You found your brother."

"Yes," he whispered. "With your help." He kissed her again, lightly. "He's with Diego. We must go. There is not much time before sunrise and we must be far away from here."

Chapter Eighteen

By sunrise they caught up with Diego and Brandon and headed northwest toward Béxar. At midmorning, they came upon an abandoned homestead. The yard stood barren with tumbleweeds blowing across the path to the smokehouse. At the far corner of the corral, a trough, empty of water, was nearly covered with weeds. Victoria nudged her horse over to a stone well in the center of the yard and peered into it. Water glistened in the bottom.

She dearly hoped they would stop for a while. She couldn't go much farther without rest and wondered how Brandon had made it this far in his condition. Jake had quieted the minute she'd spoken of her love, and now he ignored her. It didn't change how she felt about him, but it hurt. And she worried about Esteban. Had Jake killed him in their escape?

Jake dismounted and opened the cottage door. Chickens clucked from inside and then raced madly into the yard, flapping their wings in mock bravery. "We'll take a rest here," Jake said. He grasped Victoria by her waist to help her down from her mount. With the horse's warm belly behind her and Jake's intense gaze looking down on her, she thought for a moment he would kiss her again.

Instead he turned and helped his brother from his horse. Brandon's legs collapsed under him. Jake caught him on his slide to the ground, hoisting him back up while Diego rushed over and put his shoulder under Brandon's armpit. They helped him inside to the bed—a thin feather-stuffed mattress over a rope hammock. Although Victoria lifted his injured leg as gently as possible, Brandon's face paled with the pain, and his eyes closed the second his head hit the mattress.

He was younger than Jake. Slender to the point of being lanky, but just as tall. Victoria compared them, noting similarities in their features—the long straight nose and high cheekbones, the piercing blueness of their eyes. But where Brandon was slighter of build, Jake had filled out, with broad shoulders and strong arms to match.

"I'll get water for the horses," Jake said. "Then I'll take a look at that leg."

Victoria nodded. "Diego, if you will draw water for us, I'll look for some food."

Jake's gaze lingered on her before he left the cabin. He still wanted her. She could feel it. But something held him back. She shook the disturbing thoughts from her head. It didn't matter. Here was not the time or place. Capture by the Santanistas remained a constant threat. She turned to her task of finding something to eat.

By the time Diego returned with the bucket full of water, she'd found cornmeal and a small cloth bag of pecans. While she made *atole,* Jake tended to Brandon's injury. He cleaned it and rewrapped it with new bandages he'd made from an empty flour sack he'd discovered in the cupboard.

Brandon watched his brother's ministrations quietly—almost suspiciously, his eyes bleary with the need to sleep and yet brooding. Victoria found it hard to understand his mood. Wasn't he relieved to be away from Santa Anna's army? Wasn't he glad to see his brother after all this time?

"How is it?" she asked Jake.

"Healing."

"You sound amazed."

He grunted. "Since I know I'm not much of a doctor...I am."

Some of the tightness in her chest eased. It was so obvious how much he loved his brother. Couldn't Brandon see that?

She handed out the warm food, and they shared a tin cup filled with water to drink.

"We'll rest two hours before moving on," Jake said. "More than that will be dangerous. Get some sleep," he told Brandon.

He rose from the bed. "Victoria. Walk with me. We need to talk."

A sense of foreboding took hold of her. With a

glance at Brandon, and seeing that his eyes were already closing as he drifted into exhausted sleep, she followed Jake into the yard.

He waited by the well. "He'll be all right," he said, wonder in his voice. "I don't see how. It's a bad wound. I've seen men die from less."

"Perhaps he has more reason to live than they did."

His brow furrowed. "Maybe. There is the woman back home, Caroline. Although he hasn't spoken of her."

"You must talk with him. I don't know what is between you—why you hold back even now."

He pressed his lips together. "He's exhausted. Plus, it's complicated."

She thought he had more to say, but in the end he kept his thoughts to himself.

"I need to know, Jake…did you kill Esteban?" she asked. "I did not want to stay with him, but I don't wish him dead."

He studied her for a moment, his face unreadable, and then he opened his arms to her. Without hesitation she moved into them, closing her eyes as he held her.

"There is no way to be sure. But no, I don't think I hit him that hard."

A tremble of relief went through her.

"You cared for him, then," Jake said near her ear, his voice cautious.

She dragged in a long shuddering breath, her thoughts in turmoil. She'd known Esteban his entire life—the good and the bad. As children they'd played and teased each other at gatherings between their two families. "It is not black-and-white. It's complicated."

He sighed. "Understood. As much as I hate that answer."

He held her a moment more, long enough that she thought he was finished. She relaxed into his embrace, savoring his rugged leather scent.

"Did he hurt you?"

She stiffened in his arms.

"It won't change anything between us, Victoria. I just need to know." He drew back slightly, waiting for her answer.

She shook her head. "He did not touch me. When he realized that you had—" she struggled to voice her thoughts "—that I had lain with you, he was furious. He wanted me to be the pure woman he'd loved for so long. He did not want to dirty himself by taking me. I guess in a way he was caught between what he knew was right as a gentleman and what he wanted as a man."

"Yet he helped me escape when you bargained with that one precious part of you."

"I cannot understand it myself. Esteban is a rigid man. Change has always been hard on him. The rebellion—it has made him into two different men. He will hate me for betraying his trust now."

Jake was quiet for a moment, taking in what she'd said.

"I thought you had deceived me. All that time you

traveled with him you were in danger, and I let anger rule me."

"You couldn't have known, Jake."

He took a deep breath. "I'm not proud of myself. I should have trusted you."

"Yes," she said quietly. "You should have."

"To trust anyone or anything comes hard for me. People haven't been there for me. I don't have the generations you so proudly claim."

"I know I have been more fortunate than some."

"More fortunate than many. It makes you strong inside. I saw that at the Alamo."

If only he could see that he was also strong. It was their love that made them strong…together.

"When I was small, the man I thought was my father showered his love on Brandon."

"The man you *thought* was your father?"

"He knew my mother was with child before marrying her. He loved her and married her, giving me a name but nothing more, nothing of himself."

"Your mother—I'm sure she loved you."

"But not enough to stay. She left when I was twelve."

"Do you know why?" Victoria asked.

He shook his head. "She told me she couldn't try anymore. She'd had enough. I remember that they argued a lot behind closed doors. That's how I learned I wasn't his. Everything fell into place then."

"You overheard it?" Her heart went out to the boy he'd been. "You must have been so hurt."

"Actually, I was angry. I lashed out at both of

them. They had betrayed me. Both of them in their own way. Things got much worse after she left. I finally took off when I was seventeen."

"That was their problem and it painted every part of your life—even how things were with Brandon. But that part's better now."

Jake blew out a breath, looking over her head to the cabin. "Yes. At least we have a chance. A start. I've tried to protect the people I care for—you, Brandon—and yet when it came down to what really mattered, I didn't have control over any of it."

"None of us do. We just do what we can."

"I've failed at every turn. In a big way," he said flatly. He studied her face, stroking her cheek with his rough thumb. "And still you have been there for me. I just couldn't see it until now."

She turned into his palm and kissed it, watching him swallow hard. Something else bothered him.

"What if a child comes from our union? What then?" he asked.

"Besides forcing you to marry me? I would do the best I could in raising it. I would love it."

"But what if things had turned out differently? What if Esteban was the one who took it to raise and gave it his name?"

So that's what worried him. He likened this to his life—what happened with him and his mother. "Even if the child had the bluest of eyes like its father, I would never leave it, Jake. Never. I promise you this."

He stared hard at her. "I believe you. You would love it as fiercely as you do your land."

She smiled. "Oh, much more than that."

"How could I have been so blind?" He curled her into his arms, holding her close.

A contented sigh rippled through her. She could feel his love pulsing with each heartbeat. Things would be all right now. Whatever came, they'd work it out together. "I haven't made it easy for you. I see that now. We are both so different."

He brushed his lips against her brow. His voice thoughtful, he said, "So you've figured out that many things are shades of gray."

"As you warned me from the start."

"A hard lesson."

"But a necessary one."

"I must ask a favor." He stepped back from her and took both of her hands in his. "I'd like you and Diego to take Brandon with you. Back to Juan's ranch if it is safe. If not, on to your home in Laredo. Make some of that foul-smelling ointment that works so well."

"What about you?" she asked, suddenly wary. "What are you planning?"

"I will find Houston's army. Join up with Juan."

Her heart dropped to her stomach. Not now. Not after she'd just gotten him away from danger. "You are safe now. Haven't you had enough of fighting?"

"Yes, but this safety you speak of is an illusion. If Santa Anna wins you'll never be safe, you'll never have your land back."

The blood drained from her head. He was serious! She felt her world spin out of control. "No," she whispered.

"I must do this, Victoria," he said urgently. "I need to do this for you. For us. Please try to understand."

"You don't have to prove anything to me, Jake."

He squinted against the sunlight, his gaze sharp. "I do. And I have to prove it to myself.

"Victoria. You've already proven your love to me many times over. You left the Alamo when you wanted to stay, because you knew what I would do. You pleaded with Esteban to help me escape. I don't deserve your love. And I can't accept it. Not until I do some proving of my own."

Her heart broke. How much luck could one man have? Surely his—surely theirs—had run out by now. Now when he finally understood the need to take a stand for what he believed in, she would lose him. He'd never return.

A sob escaped before she could cover her mouth with her hands. She understood. God help her. She did understand. But she didn't want him to go. She couldn't bear to lose him again. This would be the end. She felt it in her heart. She turned away from him as frustration built inside.

"Victoria." He placed his hand on her shoulder.

She jerked from his touch, unable to bear it. He was leaving her again! How much was she expected to endure?

"Victoria…" He tried again.

"No, Jake, don't say any word! I will see to Brandon, but do not expect more from me." No longer able to trust her voice, she turned from him and walked to the edge of the yard. Staring out across the prairie, she murmured a prayer for strength and Jake's safety, knowing she'd repeat it constantly until they were together again.

"I've been a nursemaid long enough," Diego argued as he and Jake saddled the horses. "I want to go, too."

"I have to do this, and I'm the stronger fighter. If I don't do this now, I will never be able to stay here or live with myself. Not after what happened at the Alamo."

Diego worked the bit back into the gelding's mouth. "You have changed, Anglo. Before, you did not want to fight. It did not matter so much to you."

"It is everything now," Jake answered.

"Don't you think I feel the same?" His chin trembled with suppressed anger. "I have done what Juan asked of me. I am ready to fight now."

Jake held his gaze. He understood how Diego felt. Completely.

"I will do as you ask. But once your brother and Victoria are safe do not be surprised if you see me again." He turned to ready the other horses, his movements short and jerky.

Jake strode back inside the cabin. Brandon rose on one elbow from the mattress, still groggy from his short nap.

"We can't stay any longer. Patrols might be out looking for us as it is."

"I won't slow you down." Brandon sat up, wincing when his feet thudded against the dirt floor. He tucked a strand of dark blond hair behind his ear and then stared out the open door to where Victoria waited by her horse. "What is it with her?"

Jake followed his gaze and for a moment was lost in drinking in the sight of her. Nothing fancy about her now—her dark brown skirt was functional for riding and she wore a long leather duster, most likely a gift from Esteban. A dark hat covered her hair that was pulled back in a loose thick braid down her back. Yet as diminutive as she appeared, he knew the fire that was her. "I might as well be a moth," he murmured to himself.

When he turned back to his brother, Brandon had an amused look on his face—the first Jake had seen since they were young.

"So you have found that you are not immune."

Jake scowled, uncomfortable with having his thoughts read so easily, even if it was his brother.

"It's about time a woman got under that thick hide you grew since Mother left."

"Mother didn't have anything to do with it. I just wised up is all."

"Right," Brandon said, a sardonic lift to his brow.

Jake's jaw tightened. "You'd be smart to take notes. Caroline had as much to do with your leaving Charleston as I did."

Brandon scowled. "She doesn't figure into any of this."

"Oh, yes she does. She played us both for fools. Didn't Father warn us—"

"Father didn't have women all figured out, as much as he thought he did."

Jake snorted.

"No. I asked him once—after you left."

Jake stopped cold. Brandon was talking about more than Caroline, more than a woman's betrayal. How long had he known Jake wasn't a Dumont?

"Give me some credit. Don't you think I could tell he treated you differently? He had no patience for you."

Sure, Jake remembered. He just was surprised to hear Brandon admit to it out loud. "What did he say?"

"He tried to feel the same about you as he did me. He just couldn't. He knew down deep that it wasn't your fault. It ate away at him until it destroyed anything he felt for Mother."

Jake dragged in a deep breath. "Well, she finally got free of that situation when she left us." He started packing again, stashing the sack of cornmeal into a leather pouch.

"That was her answer when Father couldn't forgive her. And yours, too," Brandon said, making Jake pause. "You're leaving now, just like you did back then."

He spun around and faced Brandon. "It's not the same." The intensity in his voice rolled over them both.

"I've got ears. I heard you talking outside."

"I'm not running away from anyone now. And I'm not thinking only of myself as you have accused me of in the past. I'm running *to* something. Something important."

Brandon's expression became speculative. "Why her, Jake? Why now?"

He took a deep breath. His brother deserved the truth. "I love her," he said awkwardly.

Brandon studied him. "And she is worth the risk?"

Jake raised his chin defiantly. So he cared. He was putting his heart on the line. She was worth it. "All of it."

"Why are you going to fight, then? You're not making any sense. Why not come back to Béxar with us now? She wants you to."

Jake paced the short room. How much should he say? How much did he understand himself? "I want to marry her. Before another sunset if she'll have me. But I can't. Not the way things stand now."

"I don't understand."

"I'm not sure I do, either. But I know I have to join the fight. It's not because of her land. For me, it's never been because of land. Victoria is worth it, and that makes her land worth it. I'll do whatever it takes to prove to her I'll be there from now on to protect her and her home."

"You should tell her."

Jake shook his head. "I can't be sure I'll make it back alive. I don't have your fancy medical bag to save my skin this time."

His brother rose awkwardly to his feet. "Still, given that, you should tell her. She should know how you feel."

"This'll prove things—things that need proving to both of us." He squared his shoulders and met his brother's gaze. "Will you watch out for her until I come back?"

The air seemed to rush from the room as he waited for Brandon's answer.

"She can be a challenge. Getting us out of Goliad is only one example."

Brandon glanced out the open door to where Victoria saddled her horse. "What if you don't return? What then?"

Jake took a deep breath. "Make sure she gets my part of the inheritance."

Brandon's attention snapped back to him.

"I know it's a sore point between you and me. I didn't come after you because of the money, Brandon. You're my brother. The only family I've got." He stopped as he struggled against the emotion that clotted his throat. "I doubt Father left any of it to me, but if he did, I want it to help Victoria and Diego get back on their feet."

"All right, Jake. You have my word."

Jake felt as if a weight had been removed from his back. He held out his hand, ready to shake on it. "It's settled, then," he said quietly.

Brandon looked at his hand, hesitated a moment and then gripped it hard. "Thanks for coming for me, Jake. I was ready to give up. I said some things I'm not proud of."

"That makes two of us. Things happened in Charleston that I'd rather forget also." He met Brandon's gaze and took a deep breath. "It's in the past. Forgotten. You're my brother. I won't lose you again."

Brandon leaned heavily on Jake's arm and they walked out into the bright daylight to the waiting horses. Jake helped his brother up onto the mustang and then checked the cinch. They shook hands once more.

Brandon topped their clasped hands with his free one. "What you said in there—" he looked to the small shelter "—about us being brothers. I feel the same way. I won't lose you again. Or run. Godspeed, Jake."

Looking into Brandon's eyes, Jake felt as if he'd come full circle with the brother he'd known years before. For the first time in more than ten years he felt peace where his brother was concerned.

He turned to Victoria. Not caring that he had an audience, he pushed back her hat brim and kissed her with all the longing he felt inside, kissed her until he felt her start to sink as her knees gave way and he tasted her tears. He pulled back then, knowing deep inside that she was still his, would always be his and he could trust it.

"Be safe, Victoria."

Her chin trembled. "Come back to me, Jake."

He memorized her face in that moment—the aristocratic nose, the dimples in her cheeks, the love in her eyes. He'd take the image with him and knew it would carry him through whatever he had to do.

He helped her on her horse and handed her the reins. With a smack to the horse's rump, he sent them off, watching them until they disappeared across the rolling prairie. Then turning, he mounted Fury and wheeled him around toward the east—to Gonzales and Juan and his destiny.

Chapter Nineteen

April 21, 1836 ~ San Jacinto

Concealed in the line of tall oaks, Juan, Jake and Diego watched as, a mile away, a contingent of Mexican soldiers marched across the far edge of the prairie. Weary and spent, their blue uniforms now faded to drab shades of gray, they stumbled into Santa Anna's camp.

"They're moving slow," Juan observed.

"More reinforcements," Jake grumbled. "We keep waiting while their numbers grow." He glanced over at General Houston to see if he'd taken note of the Mexicans. The general stood under a magnolia tree talking to Deaf Smith, every so often glancing up to scrutinize the terrain and Santa Anna's encampment.

Jake turned and climbed down the small embankment to the river. It had been a month of retreating, as far as he was concerned. He hadn't joined up only to run again.

For all he knew, it could be another week of running from the Mexican army before they made their stand. "What is he thinking? Santa Anna is nearly upon us."

"He has his reasons," Juan replied, eyeing the Mexican tents with a seasoned eye. "Do not be so quick to jump to conclusions about him…or his tactics."

"But we are ready."

Juan gave a frustrated smile, his dark eyes tired. "We have been ready, Dumont. The timing was not right."

Jake slouched against a large boulder and leaned his head back, soaking up the warmth of the sun from the rock. Gray light filtered through the trees, revealing a bull snake slithering through the grass near his boot. He moved his leg, and the snake took off into the brush.

Some of the good things to come from all this— besides knowing Victoria—were the friendships he'd formed with Juan and Diego.

He thought of Victoria then. He wanted to see her—needed to be with her. When had the thought of being with her made everything else pale in comparison? When had she become *home* to him? Damn it all, he was losing sleep over her!

"You, there!"

Jake jumped up from the ground like a piston. His friends joined him as Deaf Smith approached with a purposeful air. Jake couldn't contain the slight buzz he felt. Maybe something was happening. At last.

"General wants to see you, Seguín. Diego."

Juan nodded. He met Jake's gaze, holding it for a second before turning and striding toward Houston, twenty rods away.

"You." Smith got Jake's attention, handing him an ax and mumbling something about the odds being better than the Alamo. "Get your horse and come with me. We have a bridge to sink."

Jake mounted Fury and followed Smith as they joined three other men at the start of a trail marked by wagon ruts. It was eight miles back to Vince's Bridge—the same bridge that the newly arrived Mexican regiment had so recently crossed over. Jake supposed that Houston wanted to eliminate the arrival of any further "guests" to whatever he had planned.

As he neared the bridge and Jake had the chance to survey the marshlike lay of the land, he realized something else and a cold premonition built inside. In destroying the bridge and trapping the Santanistas, Houston also cut off the one avenue the Texians could use for escape. He took a deep breath. This was it. They were going to make a stand! But was it folly or was it genius?

He met Smith's gaze and realized the man knew what was happening, too. Jake's grip on his ax tightened. They had a chance to defeat the small contingent of soldiers that rested across the field. It was the four thousand Mexicans led by Cos and Urrea quickly closing ranks that would slaughter them if they remained in one place.

He expected to feel that urge to escape—even waited for it. But it didn't come. He was ready. The time had come to stand and fight. He did this for Victoria's land and for the new Territory of Texas, too; for Brandon, who would have been here but for his injury; and for Juan and Diego, who had become brothers of heart if not brothers of blood. He squared his shoulders. Whether he lived or died on this field today, he'd prove himself to Victoria and he'd honor the love she carried for him.

He held the ax high. Time to head across to the other side of the bridge and tear it down.

Chapter Twenty

Brandon hobbled into the cabin and leaned his walking stick against the wall. Victoria turned back to her satchel, open on the bed. "I'm almost finished packing." She snapped the maroon dress she held in her hands—the one she'd worn the night of the fandango—and folded it carefully into a small bundle. A tear she'd tried desperately to hold back splattered onto the material making a dark wet stain.

Her heart wasn't in this.

"We have to go," Brandon said, coming to sit on the bed and stretch out his injured leg. "I promised Jake and Diego."

"But what if he returns and we are gone?"

Brandon's gaze darted around the one-room cabin. "He'll figure it out. It's not safe to stay here. Everyone has left Béxar. The fever has killed so many."

She swallowed hard. The evidence had been

ghastly—the bones of men and horses in the river—picked clean by the buzzards that still circled overhead.

"I know, and I am anxious to see my home again. Mama and Father will be worried sick about me. It's just that—" Her voice trailed off in a choked whisper and she opened her eyes wide as she felt the sting of tears.

"He's doing this for you, Victoria. Jake wants you to have your land. You must return to claim it or all his actions, all his fighting will be worthless."

"I keep hoping he'll come back. I want to be here when he does."

"I'm sure he'll find you."

"He never actually promised."

A quirky half grin lit Brandon's face, so like Jake's it made Victoria's heart flip. "Diego was right—you do demand a lot from a man."

She glared at him. She wasn't in a mood to be teased.

Understanding lit Brandon's eyes. "Victoria. Jake didn't have to promise. It's in everything he's done up to now. You know he's not much for words—not where it counts."

She drew in a breath. "I suppose you are right." She stuffed her dress into the satchel and pulled the drawstring tight. "All finished, then. I'm ready to leave."

He took the bag and, grabbing his hat from the peg and his walking stick, he headed through the door.

Victoria picked up the pan from the hearth and

walked out into the bright sunlight. She dumped the dirty water into the yard, startling a young rabbit nibbling on the grass near the door. The wind rustled the new leaves on the cottonwoods. Spring was here. A time to begin again.

She squared her shoulders and stepped down from the porch. Brandon stood frozen at the entrance to the barn, his face turned toward the line of trees edging the clearing.

Victoria followed his gaze.

Three men on horseback broke through the stand of pines. They were too far away to make out their characteristics, but she knew them by the way they sat their horses. Two black-haired and one…lighter, with streaks of gold.

The pan slipped from her fingers and clattered onto the wooden steps. "Jake!" she mouthed, her throat suddenly dry. He'd come!

He looked right at her and reined his horse, urging it into a fast gallop and pulling up short in front of her. Sliding from Fury in one fluid move, he crossed the distance between them, his blue gaze drinking her in as if she were the only important thing to him on earth.

He enveloped her in his strong arms. She melted against his hard frame, holding him tight, her heart pounding.

"Victoria," he breathed, and then leaned down to kiss her fiercely. "At last."

When he let her go, he kept one arm possessively around her waist as Brandon stepped up beside them.

"Welcome back, Jake." Brandon moved in to hug him hard, slapping his back.

A smile of sheer happiness split Jake's face as he checked the way his brother moved on his injured leg and then hugged him back. "You're looking well."

"Better," Brandon said, his face shifting into a grin. "Still stiff. But it's a whole lot better than the alternative. And Victoria here makes a good nurse."

"Victoria is it now?" Jake teased, but his gaze remained warm and steadfast on her and she saw not one hint of doubt or suspicion in their blue depths.

She couldn't take her eyes off him, either. He'd shaved recently—a small scab had formed where he'd nicked his jaw. Remembering his words about chafing her skin, she wondered if he had designs for tonight. Warmth rushed up her cheeks as she anticipated such a time together.

Brandon backed up as the second rider pulled up and dismounted.

"Diego!" Victoria cried out and threw her arms around him. He murmured a greeting in her ear and then she felt him let go with one arm and shake Brandon's hand behind her.

Juan dropped from his mount and stepped forward.

"I believe you've met Captain Seguín," Jake said to his brother. "You've been staying in his cabin here and on his land."

Brandon shook Juan's hand. "Thank you for your hospitality."

Juan nodded. "Señor Dumont. Your brother speaks

well of you." He glanced at Victoria and then turned to face her.

"Welcome home, Juan," she said, her vision misty. All three were whole. All three had returned. The months of worry and separation finally had come to an end. She could barely contain her joy. But Juan's face was solemn for such a happy occasion, making her pause. "What is it?" she asked.

Quietly he withdrew a scrap of heavy blue material from his saddlebag and handed it to her. Attached to the fabric was a gold tasseled epaulet and pinned to it was a gold ring—one she recognized.

She didn't need to say the word as her gaze met Juan's.

"This is for you," he said, and then he reached to the other side of his horse and pulled a saber from its scabbard. "He asked that you give this to his parents the next time you visit them."

"Esteban is dead?" The words came out in a whisper.

Juan nodded. "He sustained injuries at San Jacinto too serious to heal."

Conflicting emotions battled within her. She was glad to learn his death had not come from Jake's hand—and sorry it had come at all. Memories of when they were children and memories of him as an officer. Once, he had been her friend. The war had changed that.

Jake moved close and she felt his hands on her shoulders, steadying her. "If you wish, I'll see that his family receives it."

She swallowed hard and nodded.

Jake stood by quietly, and she sensed the strength of his support. Grateful for it, she drew in a shuddering breath and turned, placing her hand on his chest. "You came back."

He covered her hand with his, keeping it close. "Had to. *Te llevas mi corazon contigo.*"

You carry my heart with you. A smile tilted her lips. "Your Spanish is improving."

"Darn right, it is."

"I'd say that's worth at least five kisses."

He nodded once. "Standard payment. I'll accept it."

"Certainly—" She glanced at Juan and Diego, noting they watched the proceedings with interest. "Perhaps later."

"Then tell me how many I get for this one. *Te quiero y ya estoy listo.*"

I love you and I intend to marry you. At once thrilled and stunned at his words, she could only stare at him. Yet his bluntness in front of everyone irritated her. "Just like that? Without asking properly?"

Jake backed up, glancing from Juan to Brandon. They were grinning. "What the—"

"Did you even ask Juan for my hand like a proper suitor? That is how it is done here, you know."

"Look. Victoria…" Jake fingered the brim of his felt hat. "I talked to Juan about this a long time ago, in Gonzales."

"Gonzales? You mean before we made—"

He coughed, interrupting her. "Uh. Yes."

"Oh." She was speechless. He'd wanted to marry her since then? She looked sharply at Juan. "And my cousin gave his consent?"

Juan shook his head. "No, not then. He was not good enough for you. But after—in Goliad and in San Jacinto—he proved himself."

She sighed with relief. Juan approved of this match. It meant much to her that Juan would stand by her decision. He would smooth the way with her parents.

"In that case, there is more that must be said," she said.

His brow quirked up. "Go on…"

"I won't leave my land, Jake. Can you be happy here in Tejas?"

"It's wilder and tougher, but that suits me."

"Yes," she said, appraising him and noting how he'd gained back much of the weight he'd lost among the Santanistas and how the gleam was back in his eyes. "I think it does suit you."

"I'll do anything to keep you by my side, Victoria. It took me a while but I think I've finally proved that—to you and to myself. I want what you have, what you can give me—strong roots. For me and for our children."

"Then, yes. I'll marry you, Jake Dumont."

A large grin split his face. "I'll never let you regret it." He kissed her soundly, sealing his words in her heart.

"I won't let you, either, *mi amor.*"

He moved to mount Fury, shoving his foot in the

stirrup and grasping the saddle horn. "I'll head back to Béxar and find a priest."

"*Amigo*. Wait," Diego said, placing a hand on Jake's shoulder.

A smile threatened as Victoria shook her head. "Not here, Jake. At my hacienda, with my parents and grandparents and cousins."

With a disconcerting look, he glanced from Brandon to Juan and then back at her. "You are serious? A big wedding?"

She took his hands in hers.

"I may need to learn more Spanish. Exactly how many people are we talking about?"

"Just my closest relatives and friends. Perhaps a hundred or so."

His face paled. "That big?"

Bursting with happiness, Victoria smiled up at him. "As big as the Republic of Tejas."

* * * * *

Chapter 1

October
New York City

Nicole Masters was sitting cross-legged on her sofa while a cold autumn rain peppered the windows of her fourth-floor apartment. She was poking at the ice cream in her bowl and trying not to be in a mood.

Six weeks ago, a simple trip to her neighborhood pharmacy had turned into a nightmare. She'd walked into the middle of a robbery. She never even saw the man who shot her in the head and left her for dead. She'd survived, but some of her senses had not. She was dealing with short-term memory loss and a tendency to stagger. Even though she'd been told the problems were most likely temporary, she waged a daily battle with depression.

Her parents had been killed in a car wreck when she was twenty-one. And except for a few friends—and most recently her boyfriend, Dominic Tucci, who lived in the apartment right above hers—she was alone. Her doctor kept reminding her that she should be grateful to be alive, and on one level she knew he was right. But he wasn't living in her shoes.

If she'd been anywhere else but at that pharmacy when the robbery happened, she wouldn't have died twice on the way to the hospital. Instead of being grateful that she'd survived, she couldn't stop thinking of what she'd lost.

But that wasn't the end of her troubles. On top of everything else, something strange was happening inside her head. She'd begun to hear odd things: sounds, not voices—at least, she didn't think it was voices. It was more like the distant noise of rapids—a rush of wind and water inside her head that, when it came, blocked out everything around her. It didn't happen often, but when it did, it was frightening, and it was driving her crazy.

The blank moments, which is what she called them, even had a rhythm. First there came that sound, then a cold sweat, then panic with no reason. Part of her feared it was the beginning of an emotional breakdown. And part of her feared it wasn't—that it was going to turn out to be a permanent souvenir of her resurrection.

Frustrated with herself and the situation as it stood, she upped the sound on the TV remote. But instead of *Wheel of Fortune,* an announcer broke in with a special bulletin.

"This just in. Police are on the scene of a kidnapping that occurred only hours ago at The Dakota. Molly Dane, the six-year-old daughter of one of Hollywood's blockbuster stars, Lyla Dane, was taken by force from the family apartment. At this time they have yet to receive a ransom demand. The housekeeper was seriously injured during the abduction, and is, at the pres-

ent time, in surgery. Police are hoping to be able
to talk to her once she regains consciousness. In
the meantime, we are going now to a press conference with Lyla Dane."

Horrified, Nicole stilled as the cameras went live to
where the actress was speaking before a bank of micro-
phones. The shock and terror in Lyla Dane's voice were
physically painful to watch. But even though Nicole
kept upping the volume, the sound continued to fade.

Just when she was beginning to think something
was wrong with her set, the broadcast suddenly
switched from the Dane press conference to what
appeared to be footage of the kidnapping, beginning
with footage from inside the apartment.

When the front door suddenly flew back against the
wall and four men rushed in, Nicole gasped. Horrified,
she quickly realized that this must have been caught on
a security camera inside the Dane apartment.

As Nicole continued to watch, a small Asian
woman, who she guessed was the maid, rushed
forward in an effort to keep them out. When one of
the men hit her in the face with his gun, Nicole
moaned. The violence was too reminiscent of what
she'd lived through. Sick to her stomach, she fisted her
hands against her belly, wishing it was over, but
unable to tear her gaze away.

When the maid dropped to the carpet, the same
man followed with a vicious kick to the little woman's
midsection that lifted her off the floor.

"Oh, my God," Nicole said. When blood began to
pool beneath the maid's head, she started to cry.

As the tape played on, the four men split up in different directions. The camera caught one running down a long marble hallway, then disappearing into a room. Moments later he reappeared, carrying a little girl, who Nicole assumed was Molly Dane. The child was wearing a pair of red pants and a white turtleneck sweater, and her hair was partially blocking her abductor's face as he carried her down the hall. She was kicking and screaming in his arms, and when he slapped her, it elicited an agonized scream that brought the other three running. Nicole watched in horror as one of them ran up and put his hand over Molly's face. Seconds later, she went limp.

One moment they were in the foyer, then they were gone.

Nicole jumped to her feet, then staggered drunkenly. The bowl of ice cream she'd absentmindedly placed in her lap shattered at her feet, splattering glass and melting ice cream everywhere.

The picture on the screen abruptly switched from the kidnapping to what Nicole assumed was a rerun of Lyla Dane's plea for her daughter's safe return, but she was numb.

Before she could think what to do next, the doorbell rang. Startled by the unexpected sound, she shakily swiped at the tears and took a step forward. She didn't feel the glass shards piercing her feet until she took the second step. At that point, sharp pains shot through her foot. She gasped, then looked down in confusion. Her legs looked as if she'd been running through mud, and she was standing in broken glass and ice cream, while a thin ribbon of blood seeped out from beneath her toes.

"Oh, no," Nicole mumbled, then stifled a second moan of pain.

The doorbell rang again. She shivered, then clutched her head in confusion.

"Just a minute!" she yelled, then tried to sidestep the rest of the debris as she hobbled to the door.

When she looked through the peephole in the door, she didn't know whether to be relieved or regretful.

It was Dominic, and as usual, she was a mess.

Nicole smiled a little self-consciously as she opened the door to let him in. "I just don't know what's happening to me. I think I'm losing my mind."

"Hey, don't talk about my woman like that."

Nicole rode the surge of delight his words brought. "So I'm still your woman?"

Dominic lowered his head.

Their lips met.

The kiss proceeded.

Slowly.

Thoroughly.

* * * * *

Be sure to look for the
AFTERSHOCK *anthology next month,*
as well as other exciting paranormal stories
from Silhouette Nocturne.
Available in October wherever books are sold.

nocturne™

NEW YORK TIMES BESTSELLING AUTHOR

SHARON SALA

JANIS REAMES HUDSON
DEBRA COWAN

AFTERSHOCK

Three women are brought to the brink of death...
only to discover the aftershock of their trauma has
left them with unexpected and unwelcome gifts of
paranormal powers. Now each woman must learn to
accept her newfound abilities while fighting for life,
love and second chances....

Available October wherever books are sold.

www.eHarlequin.com
www.paranormalromanceblog.wordpress.com

SN61796

REQUEST YOUR FREE BOOKS!

Harlequin® Historical
Historical Romantic Adventure!

2 FREE NOVELS PLUS 2 **FREE GIFTS!**

YES! Please send me 2 FREE Harlequin® Historical novels and my 2 FREE gifts (gifts are worth about $10). After receiving them, if I don't wish to receive any more books, I can return the shipping statement marked "cancel". If I don't cancel, I will receive 6 brand-new novels every month and be billed just $4.94 per book in the U.S. or $5.49 per book in Canada, plus 25¢ shipping and handling per book and applicable taxes, if any*. That's a savings of 20% off the cover price! I understand that accepting the 2 free books and gifts places me under no obligation to buy anything. I can always return a shipment and cancel at any time. Even if I never buy another book, the two free books and gifts are mine to keep forever.

246 HDN ERUM 349 HDN ERUA

Name _____ (PLEASE PRINT)

Address _____ Apt. #

City _____ State/Prov. _____ Zip/Postal Code

Signature (if under 18, a parent or guardian must sign)

Mail to the **Harlequin Reader Service:**
IN U.S.A.: P.O. Box 1867, Buffalo, NY 14240-1867
IN CANADA: P.O. Box 609, Fort Erie, Ontario L2A 5X3

Not valid to current subscribers of Harlequin Historical books.

Want to try two free books from another line?
Call 1-800-873-8635 or visit www.morefreebooks.com.

* Terms and prices subject to change without notice. N.Y. residents add applicable sales tax. Canadian residents will be charged applicable provincial taxes and GST. Offer not valid in Quebec. This offer is limited to one order per household. All orders subject to approval. Credit or debit balances in a customer's account(s) may be offset by any other outstanding balance owed by or to the customer. Please allow 4 to 6 weeks for delivery. Offer available while quantities last.

Your Privacy: Harlequin Books is committed to protecting your privacy. Our Privacy Policy is available online at www.eHarlequin.com or upon request from the Reader Service. From time to time we make our lists of customers available to reputable third parties who may have a product or service of interest to you. If you would prefer we not share your name and address, please check here.

Harlequin® Historical
Historical Romantic Adventure!

HALLOWE'EN HUSBANDS

With three fantastic stories by

Lisa Plumley
Denise Lynn
Christine Merrill

Don't miss these unforgettable
stories about three women who
experience the mysterious
happenings of Allhallows Eve
and come to discover that finding
true love on this eerie day is not
so scary after all.

Look for
HALLOWE'EN HUSBANDS

Available October
wherever books are sold.

COMING NEXT MONTH FROM

HARLEQUIN®
HISTORICAL

- **THE MAGIC OF CHRISTMAS**
  by **Carolyn Davidson, Victoria Bylin and Cheryl St.John**
  (Western)
  Three festive stories with all the seasonal warmth of the West—
  guaranteed to keep you snug from the cold this Yuletide!

- **SCANDALIZING THE TON**
  by **Diane Gaston**
  (Regency)
  Lady Lydia Wexin has been abandoned by her family and friends,
  and creditors hound her. Her husband's scandalous death has left her
  impoverished, and the gossipmongering press is whipped into a frenzy
  of speculation when it becomes clear the widow is with child. Who is
  the father? Only one man knows: Adrian Pomroy, Viscount Cavanley..

- **HALLOWE'EN HUSBANDS**
  by **Lisa Plumley, Denise Lynn, Christine Merrill**
  (Western/Medieval/Regency)
  All is not as it seems for three lucky ladies on All Hallows' Eve. The
  last thing they expect from the mystery of the night is a betrothal!

- **THE DARK VISCOUNT**
  by **Deborah Simmons**
  (Regency)
  A mysterious gothic mansion haunts Bartholomew, Viscount Townsend
  but it is also the new home of childhood friend
  Sydony Marchant. The youthful bond they once shared is lost—will o
  stolen kiss be enough to rekindle that intimacy and help them unravel
  the shadows of the past?